LIVING PASSIONATELY SERIES

BOOK ONE

Racing Desire

PAMELA H. BENDER

ISBN: 1493583336

ISBN-13: 9781493583331

Library of Congress Control Number: 2013920493

CreateSpace Independent Publishing Platform,

North Charleston, South Carolina

Acknowledgments

To those of you who have lost sleep while reading my books, I both identify with and thank you. Once the characters are fully formed, they take over my life. During the last stages of a book, I sleep in patches, a few hours at a time. Joe stands guard, making sure I eat and communicate with the living. The people in books can be so possessive. So thank you, Joe, my husband, hero and lover.

Thanks to sweet Diane Adamson, who is one of the people to whom this book is dedicated. She keeps me inspired and fixes all the mistakes that don't seem important when my heart is racing and my fingers are typing at warp speed.

Finding the perfect picture for a novel is like looking for a pearl in a barrel of oysters. I found two pearls: Anna L. Stoner, a dear friend and jewelry designer, who is studying at Savannah College of Art and Design, and her brother, Danny Stoner, a promising photographer who loves and respects both his sister and animals. It's wonderful working with talented people who are dedicated to art.

Thank you, Judy and Tad Egloff, for taking me into the world of harness racing and showing me what goes on at a horse farm before the race begins. I can still see Rowdy running up from your pond.

The Hanover Shoe Farm has allowed me to spend time in their barns asking questions and studying their magnificent horses. During the York County Fair, I was allowed to be in the barns with the horses, drivers, and grooms during the Pennsylvania Fair Sire Stakes for pacing colts. I am grateful for the gracious support of both organizations.

I would not write one word without the support of my children, their spouses, and my grandchildren. You accept the fact that having a writer for a family elder means unusual trips to strange places to research odd facts for some book. You explain the current lingo and teach me about technology. The Square has allowed me to sell books anywhere, including in grocery stores or parking lots.

Thank you, Frank Baker, for being my webpage designer and support. You're not only a great son-in-law but also a talented designer.

Last but not least, thank you to Aunt Lydia Duper, the other person to whom this book is dedicated. Your melodic voice on the other end of the phone encourages me and makes me laugh. You can speak for my dad and mom because you remember how they thought. When we talk after you read my drafts, it's like getting insight into what they would think. How can I have doubt if you approve?

Life cannot be recorded accurately if you are not grounded in love. I am blessed.

Pamela H Bender

Dedication

This book is dedicated to:

*My 92-year-old aunt, Lydia Dupler, who urged me to be bold
and fearless when I write*

and

*My best friend, cousin, muse and editor, Diane Adamson.
Without you, none of my books would have been published.*

One

Jo laughed as her mixed bulldog, Rowdy, jogged up from the pond with a bullfrog hanging from his mouth. "You're the ugliest dog in the world," she called out affectionately, urging him to her side. "The ugliest and the silliest." Rowdy snorted loudly, dropping the mashed frog by her boots. Jo reached down and playfully swatted him across his wide, brindle back. "Rowdy, you're my pal, but why don't you kill the mice in the barn or the groundhogs in the pasture?" Rowdy snorted again before rolling around on the dead frog. "What a clown," Jo remarked, as she turned away and sat on the top rung of the pasture fence.

The fierce July sun was setting, ending the suffocating day. Jo twisted her long blonde hair into two thick braids and took a deep breath. Slowly her eyes scanned her horse farm. "How I love it," she whispered, her face reflecting her pride. Her dark, brown eyes looked out toward the far pasture. The mares, all in foal, were grazing lazily on the rich Pennsylvania farmland.

Jo stretched her arms over her head. She was tired from the training session with her two-year-old colt, Jupiter, but it was a happy tired. He was almost full-grown, and his huge legs and strong muscles made him fast. Jo smiled as she ran her tongue over her parched lips. Maybe, just maybe, she daydreamed, *he'll be even faster than the stallion that fathered him.* Jo closed her eyes as she lowered her arms and slipped into her favorite daydream. She could see the track, hear the noise, and taste the sweet promise of victory. It would be Jupiter and she crossing the finish line ahead of all the other pacers. In September, at the York Fair, they'd finally prove the strength of both their breeding. Jo opened her eyes and shivered in excitement. The daydream had existed for two generations. Now she felt it was close to becoming a reality. The son of her dad's beloved stallion would bring home the winner's cup.

Jo's eyes fell on the form of her other two-year-old, Little Girl. The same stallion sired the filly, but this horse was thin and restless. Still, there was the promise of untapped speed, despite her shorter legs and smaller body. *If she'd just settle down,* Jo mused, *maybe she'd gain weight. There's potential there; I can feel it.*

Jo shrugged off her thoughts and turned to watch Rowdy. "It's been a good day, hasn't it, old boy? Better days are on their way," she called over to Rowdy. The dog just snorted and continued digging a hole, the dirt flying between his bowed legs. "Rowdy, you bury frogs like normal dogs bury bones. You're just plain crazy."

The neighing of frightened horses shattered Jo's laughter. Her eyes dashed back to the mares, now running in a startled pack. Jo placed her boots on the first rail of the fence and stood up. Something was very wrong; she could feel it as vividly as she could feel the cool of the evening creeping over the farm.

"Trouble?" a voice called from behind her. Jo turned to see Ruben at the barn door. Even his aged ears had picked up the disruption on the farm he'd worked for over forty years.

"I don't know," Jo called back. "Something's got the mares skittish." She climbed one rail higher, balancing herself with her knees. She studied the horses, desperately looking for the reason they were nervous. Instinct made her spot a movement in the paddock next to them. That corral was only used for hitching the training cart up to the two-year-olds, yet something was in it. Joe's eyes strained to make out the form. Terror shot through her as she recognized the rearing animal. It was Jupiter, her precious colt!

"Oh, no!" she screamed out. "Mack must have left Jupiter alone in the hitching corral."

She was off the fence and running for her farm, her reputation, and most of all her beloved colt. The horse was flaring his nostrils, rearing up on his hind legs. She could see him getting increasingly agitated. Jupiter wanted to get to the mares, his sexual lust overwhelming his entire body. His frustrated neighing sounded like impassioned pleas meant to lure the frightened mares.

As Jo ran, her heart pounded in fear and absolute fury. Her hands balled into fists as she came to the small gully between pastures. Jo looked again, hoping to see Mack moving to distract Jupiter, but Mack wasn't there.

"That lazy ass," she cursed as she took a deep breath and headed down the gully at top speed. "He left Jupiter alone next to the mares despite all my warnings. No one can be that irresponsible. I don't care how much I need his help; he's gone. I'm firing that useless kid."

As her boots hit the dry bottom of the gully, she heard the horrible sound of bone cracking. She stopped, holding her breath and praying, "No, please no!"

Jupiter's whine of pain shattered all hope. As she ran up the other side of the gully, she prepared herself for what she knew must've happened. At the crest of the gully, her worst fears were confirmed. Jupiter's head was arched back in pain, his nostrils flared. His front legs were twisted on a fence rail, and one looked injured. The pain in his whinny sent chills up Jo's spine.

Jo ran across the field, scaled the white fence, and landed beside the frightened animal. She moved unconsciously, driven by numb panic. Her hands rubbed over Jupiter's sweating body while looking into his terrified eyes. With one swift jerk, she freed Jupiter's mangled leg while her voice softly reassured him, "It's going to be all right, boy. I'm here; steady now. Whoa there, Jupiter. I'll get you fixed up." She controlled her own hysteria, thinking only of the need of the horse she'd raised from birth.

Jo looked up and saw Ruben making his way across the field bringing a lead line with him. His gloomy face reflected his own concern. Jo answered his unspoken questions, just as she did in normal routine matters, "It's bad, Ruben. Call the vet." Her hands slid up the neck of the horse. "I can't believe old Doc isn't here. He's who we need today."

Ruben mumbled his regrets as he handed her the lead and turned for the barn. Through tear-filled eyes, Jo watched Ruben hurry back to the barn. He was getting too old for all the work and stress of the farm. That's why she had tolerated Mack's lethargy. The teenager had provided the strength that both Ruben and Jo lacked, but the price was too high. The teenager's carelessness may have just destroyed her prize colt, reputation, and dreams. Still, she called after Ruben, "Don't worry; he's going to be as good as new."

Jo's hands shook as she snapped the lead onto the bit. Carefully, she tugged on the end, pulling Jupiter toward the barn. "Come on, boy," she urged. "You'll make it."

It was a long, slow trip to the barn. Jupiter limped in pain on his three strong legs, his big, brown eyes looking at Jo for encouragement. It was just a horse and his owner painfully making their way to the barn, but in reality it was much more. Trust and love made the trip possible, friendship between two close companions. Step by step they made the exhausting journey to the shade and quiet of the big, stone barn. Somewhere, in her deepest emotions, Jo feared it was the last trip they would ever take together. Jupiter's future had been taken away from her. His fate now lay in the hands of a stranger, the new vet she'd never even met.

Jo leaned all her ninety-two pounds against the animal, straining to make him lie down on the soft, straw bedding of the stall. Jupiter was dripping with perspiration, but Jo didn't notice. She lay beside the colt and stroked him gently. "Two years," she whispered in his ear, "two years we've been together. We've come so far, dreamed so hard. Don't let me down now, Jupiter. Don't lose your fight."

The minutes hung on like hours. Jo's arms ached and her head pounded with frustrated tension. "Where's that vet?" she called out through the empty barn. She was angry—angry at Mack for being so careless, angry with the vet for taking so long, angry at fate for once again draining the hope from her life.

Just then, two low voices could be heard through the open doors. Jo strained to listen, "Is that you, Ruben?" Is that vet here yet?"

"Yes," Ruben answered, in his usual few words.

Jo stayed crouched beside her colt. Suddenly she didn't want a stranger to disturb the chestnut horse beside her. She didn't want him confirming her greatest fears. Jo kept her eyes on the horse.

"Move over," a deep voice demanded. "Give me room." He entered the stall as if he owned it. Jo resented his attempt at control. Her eyes worked over to the stranger's boots. They were dirty and well worn. Her glance traveled up his faded jeans, noting they were work pants, not worn for style. They passed up to his chest, finding it broad and thick and the muscles apparent through the thin, cotton shirt. She stared at the tan arms that laid his black bag beside her feet. They were twisted ropes of muscle and hair. Still she didn't look at his face; she didn't want that yet. She just wanted his hands to work a miracle on Jupiter's leg and then leave. Her eyes went back to the horse.

He crouched beside her, his presence filling the stall. Jupiter reacted just as Jo had. He raised his head and flared his nostrils, warning him away. Jo leaned past the stranger to stroke the horse's head; "It's all right, boy. Whoa there." She forced the man back, one hand shoving against his chest.

"You're in my way, little girl," his voice said firmly. "Better leave now."

It was a gentle command, one that came from a person who knows how protective a human can feel over his/her horse. Still, Jo bristled at his words. She realized she must indeed look like a grief-filled girl in pigtails. She moved to a spot near Jupiter's hind-quarter. "I'm not leaving," she said softly.

The man sighed loudly but dismissed her from his mind. He was absorbed in the animal before him. It was he who now reached past Jo. He gently pushed her back as he grabbed for the colt's leg. His arm stopped for one brief moment as it ran across Jo's breasts. He was surprised to suddenly sense she was a woman. "Excuse me," he mumbled, embarrassed. "I need more room."

Jo moved back and stood up, feeling his eyes follow her, scanning every inch of her five-foot frame. Their brief contact disturbed her. He'd made it clear that he was alive, and curiosity now demanded that she put a face to the body. She looked at him.

His hair was the color of dark honey, his shoulders broader than they should be. His lips appeared soft, but the remainder of his facial features were bold and extremely masculine. He was a powerful man. His eyes trapped her. They were gentle and the color of blue sky. The honey-colored brows raised in admiration as he reassessed the woman standing beside him, his full lips curling into a slight smile. The look had taken only a second. It was the exchange of two strangers, taking a mere flick of time, but Jo felt it run through her body. The sensation only increased her annoyance with the man and his attitude toward both her and Jupiter. Who did this stranger think he was to come into their world and assess both of them?

He turned back to his work. His big hand grabbed the mangled leg of the colt while his fingers kneaded up the broken bones like thick vices capable of crushing the torn muscle. He held the struggling colt down with his other hand, his muscles straining against the strength of the terrified animal. What would normally take two men, he did by himself. Jo watched in silence, hoping beyond hope and numb in fear. His one hand gently released the broken leg and opened the black bag. Jo moved along the stall wall and knelt beside Jupiter's head. She took control of the horse, her hands rubbing up his neck. The man's other hand released the horse, trusting her ability to handle the colt. Quietly, he filled the needle with serum and gave the horse a shot. Jupiter raised his head in protest and then lay down again. The colt's breathing slowed and became relaxed. Jupiter was out of pain, resting comfortably. No words had been spoken, no diagnosis given, but Jo knew the silence held bad news. She rose to her feet, turning the colt over to Ruben. She walked toward the barn doors and fresh air. From behind her she could hear the man's question, "Where's the owner? Where's Jo Martin?" She knew Ruben would just nod in her direction.

Jo moved through the barn doors walking slowly toward the fence. Rowdy followed her feet, tugging at her jeans. She kicked him off, warning, "Not now, boy." She climbed on the rail and settled herself in her favorite place. Twilight was setting in. Jo scanned her farm. The fifteen mares had settled down in the pasture, the excitement forgotten. Her stallion, the father of Jupiter, pranced around in his paddock, safe from the danger his offspring had fallen prey to. Her eyes searched the field for one thing: one thing she had to see, her filly, Little Girl. She spotted her down at the pond, drinking from the clear water. *She's so small,* Jo thought, and so thin. *She's not strong enough to carry the load.* Jo's hand darted up to her face, brushing back a tear. The colt had been the one strong enough to prove the worth of his sire. He had the male strength to beat out the other horses and make a name for all of them. Little Girl was much smaller and just a filly. She was like the woman she was named after, Jo herself, built small. Jo shivered at the thought, their similarities suddenly clear.

Jo heard Rowdy growling behind her. She knew he would be nipping at the stranger's boots, biting his jeans. She was glad. He was the bearer of bad news, and Jo appreciated Rowdy slowing the vet's progress "Get back, you ugly mutt," the man commanded. Jo just stared out across her farm holding onto the precious moments before her horse's prognosis was announced.

His footsteps came faster now, crunching on the dirt path behind her. She felt the fence creak under her body as he pulled himself up on the rail. Jo felt his presence as he lowered himself to sit alongside her, a few inches apart. Still, quiet filled the air. She braced herself for the inevitable question, and then it came. "What happened?" he asked in a slow, southern drawl.

She fought back the humiliation and answered honestly, "The colt got hung up on the fence, trying to get to the mares."

Jo waited for the sly comments, tensed for the tone of disbelief. Nothing came, just silence. She calmed down. Jo knew his eyes were scanning her farm, assessing her ability to absorb the loss of the colt. Few words were needed; the horses were the best criteria for appraisal. Expert eyes could assess how well a horse farm was doing by just running up and down the lines of the animals that were raised there. Trivial conversations were cut to the bone with horse people. The strength of your breeding stock told how well you were doing, how hard you were working, and how close you were to getting the horse trainer's dream of owning a field of strong winners.

The stallion neighed into the cooling, night air. Jo and the vet watched quietly as Ruben crossed over to him and led him into the barn for the night. The stallion moved with fluid grace. Just a slight limp gave testimony to a prior injury not unlike his son's. "Is that the stud?" the man asked.

Jo answered with pride, "Yes." She shifted her weight "The mare the colt's out of is a valuable one. I only have four mares of my own, but they're all good horses with fast track records" She was proud of her horses, of her life.

"What's the stallion's time?" he asked calmly. It always came back to the bloodline. Horses were only as valuable as the stock they were bred from. They carried the reputation of their parents with them. It was a caste system that was almost impossible to break out of except for the few with speed and racing desire all their own. One fast, winning horse could legitimize his parents as valuable breeding stock. He could crush the system and bring him-self and his family into a class all their own. *Jupiter would have done this*, Jo thought. *Jupiter would have done this for all of us.* The image of the horse lying crippled and in pain flashed through her mind. Jo shivered.

The tension began to seep back into Jo's body. "The stallion's not track-proven," she sighed. "He was injured first time out, but he would have won. He was faster than any horse in the race."

She felt the man shift his weight. She sensed his doubts. Jo knew he probably subscribed to the popular opinion that mating an unproven stud to a valuable mare was sheer folly. Jo braced herself for his disapproval, but she was met with silence.

"Any other two-year-olds to rely on?" he asked, continuing the appraisal.

"Just the filly in the field by the pond," Jo said, as her eyes focused on Little Girl's trim body. She felt like protecting her against the scrutiny of this stranger's eyes.

"Who's her sire?" he asked, casually.

Jo gripped her hand against the top rail of the fence, hating his questions, but understanding his interest. "The same stallion," she answered, spitting the words out quickly, offering no explanation.

"You bred two mares to the same unproven stallion?" His ques-tion's tone was disbelief.

"Yes," she answered firmly. "I bred all four of my mares to him. One mare didn't take, one aborted in birth, and two produced strong stock." She didn't apologize; she didn't go into explana-tions. She just stated facts.

Again Jo waited for laughing recriminations. Nothing came. Together they watched as Ruben returned to the field to lead

Little Girl to her stall. Ruben was taking no chances with the filly. She would be placed safely in the barn for the night.

"Why don't you call me *Brad*", the voice asked politely

"Then call me *Jo*," she answered, turning her head to meet his stare. Their eyes locked on each other, two strangers joined by the knowledge of a pain they must share, Jupiter's pain.

His face seemed gentler now, the tension of the horse's immediate needs removed. Jo decided that he was a handsome man, built like a Clydesdale horse—thick and stocky. He was made for hard work and power, not like so many other men she had seen. Where they were tall, long-legged, and trim, he was shorter; around 5'9" with thick muscles covering his broad build. He looked like a man reared around horses, one who worked in barns cleaning stalls and loading heavy bales of hay. He didn't look like a vet. Somehow Jo had always pictured them as being more cerebral than physical, more thoroughbred than Clydesdale. Her lips twisted into a faint smile. She was grading him like the livestock she lived among. Her incorrigible sense of humor was giving her refuge, even during this catastrophe. Jo turned away, grateful for the dark that was coming down like a blanket around them. He was disturbing, this Clydesdale male, very different and disrupting.

"The colt has a compound fracture." His words came like knives through the dark. They struck Jo's heart and ripped it into shreds. "I have to put him down. There's no hope."

Silence filled the air again. The man didn't go into long apologies over how he hated to do it. They weren't necessary. Anyone involved with horses loved them. Anyone dedicating his life to healing animals hated to destroy them. Jo knew this, but still anger filled her. Her eyes watched as Ruben led Little Girl toward the barn. She was so thin and just a filly. Little Girl wasn't ready to shoulder the fate of Jo's dreams, the stallion's reputation and the farm's security. She was too skittish, too insecure on the track. "No," Jo said softly "Not now."

She heard the sigh of disapproval; she knew he felt her incompetent and emotional in her decisions. Jo understood his impatience with her.

"Is there someone else who advises you?" he asked slowly. "How about your dad, or brother, or someone?" He was searching for a male to deal with, looking for a stronger sprit capable of facing the truth. It infuriated Jo, so she dug her nails into the fence to help control her anger.

"No, my dad's dead. I don't have any brothers or sisters if you're desperate enough to wonder about that. You're stuck with me. I call all the shots on this farm," her eyes darted back to him, daring him to push the issue further.

He stared into them, reading the brown pools of determination. Her chin rose up proudly. She looked like a contrast in statement. Her hair was still braided into two thick pigtails, her small frame helping to make her look childish. Only the full curve of her firm busts and the flash of anger in her eyes attested to her experience. His lips moved into a slight grin. She might be small in build, but he sensed she was a spitfire when she needed to be.

Brad slipped down from the fence. "The colt's going to be in pain," he added in one last attempt. "I hate to see a horse go through needless pain."

Her eyes narrowed. "So do I, but maybe it won't be useless. Maybe tomorrow his leg will look better." Jo fought to hold onto her colt for at least one more night. Jupiter might have enough strength to heal. He might still make her dreams come true.

Her eyes dared Brad to protest, until she heard Rowdy growling. Her face changed and she flashed a sarcastic smile toward Brad. "Where did you put your leather bag?" she asked casually.

"By the barn door," Brad answered, his face showing his confusion.

Jo smiled broadly now, unable to cover her amusement.

"Well, I suspect my dog is in the process of chewing it to bits. He hates bullfrogs and leather."

Brad moved his gaze to the barn. Rowdy was dragging the bag across the yard, gnawing busily through the leather and growling in absolute concentration. Brad moved quickly, like a powerful workhorse running to the feed. She watched in amusement as he tugged the bag from Rowdy's jaws and picked up the medicine and needles that had fallen out of the holes already made. *Maybe Rowdy's not so useless,"* she thought, pleased. *He managed to stop that disagreeable discussion.*

Jo slid off the fence and rested her elbows against it, laughter seeping into her body, washing away the pain for a few minutes. While Brad gathered his things, Rowdy walked calmly over to his jeep and lifted his leg to pee on the tire. The jeep was now marked. Rowdy would do that every time it came back to the farm. As Brad pulled out of the drive, she knew there would be many opportunities for Rowdy to revisit that tire. She only prayed that the next time the jeep brought Brad to her farm, he could give her good news.

Brad stood over Jo, staring down at her thoughtfully. Her long, blond hair fell around her pillow like a thick, rich mane; her soft, pink lips were turned up in a slight smile, as if she were lost in a delightful dream that gave her pleasure. His eyes examined the rise of her breasts under the thin tee shirt she now wore. They roamed to her tiny waist and slim hips, now encased in a fresh pair of faded jeans. He smiled as he noticed that she slept with her boots on. She was ready to get up at a moment's notice. She was different, this woman before him. She was small, but now he could see her toned arms and the muscles in her back. He had seen the flash of pride in her deep, brown eyes and in her hands as she controlled the huge livestock. She was unconventional, holding to no set patterns, and he wanted this woman. He suddenly wanted her more than he had wanted any woman in his life.

Jo moved slightly, the cot creaking under her. She was used to sleeping in the barn with the noise of animals around her. She'd done it many times. Still, something disturbed Jo. Her senses picked up new vibrations, and a chill ran through her. She withdrew from her dream and forced herself back into the real world. Jo opened her eyes.

He stood above her like a characterization of a western outlaw. His hair fell onto his forehead; his hands were clenched into fists. Jo felt his eyes on her body. They seemed to burn into her flesh as they roamed every inch of her. The once gentle sky-blue eyes were now filled with sensuality and lust. Jo could feel it, just as she had felt Jupiter's desire rising for the mares. She could sense the man in this stranger taking over the gentleman.

His eyes locked onto hers, discovering that she had caught him. He didn't flinch in embarrassment. He didn't turn away from her glare. He just stared back at her in deep, concentrated study, letting Jo feel the power of his hunger.

Jo swung her feet onto the floor. Her hair flew around her like golden strands whipped into frenzy. Her chin jutted up in anger as her big, brown eyes flashed a warning, lest he act on his longing.

Brad watched her every move, a smile growing on his full lips, a spark shining in the cobalt eyes. Slowly, he crouched down beside her, staying close—closer than he should be. His muscular thighs balanced his weight; his face came even with hers. Jo watched, determined not to move back or wince. Their faces were mere inches apart. His eyes lowered from hers to the floor of the barn. "Do you always," he asked slowly, "sleep with mutts?" His eyes returned to hers.

Jo studied him carefully, her mind racing through the possible meaning of his comment. Then, suddenly, a smile came over her face. Her eyes dropped to Rowdy, who was busily snoring beneath her cot. "He's supposed to be my watchdog," she answered, laughing.

"He's not doing a very good job," Brad responded.

Jo still felt violated. He had been staring at her with abandoned interest. She raised her perfectly shaped brows in disapproval.

"Perhaps I need to get a few more dogs. What are you doing here?"

Brad rose and walked to Jupiter's stall. "I thought I'd check out the situation." His eyes returned to hers. All former emotions were erased, and he was business again "How's the colt doing?"

Jo stood up and brushed herself off, an unconscious act more meant to brush aside the stares that she had felt covering her body. Her thoughts returned to the colt. "He's slept quietly so far. Will the shot wear off soon?"

Brad moved into the stall, picked up the swollen leg, and examined it. Jupiter raised his head and then lowered it, slipping back into drugged rest. Brad walked from the stall. "I'd better stay around here now. He's going to be in pain soon." Jo kept her eyes on the colt. The leg was ballooning up. It was the worst break she'd ever seen. Doubt crept into her thoughts. The last thing she wanted to do was put Jupiter through unnecessary pain.

Brad found her thermos beside the cot and asked from behind her, "Can I have some coffee?"

"I only have one cup and it's dirty," she answered over her shoulder.

She could smell the coffee as he poured it into her cup. "I don't mind if you don't," he answered. "We can share."

Jo turned to watch him as he walked over to her side, drinking a long swig. His eyes came to hers; there seemed to be a sudden intimacy between them. Jo smiled, the devil in her taking over. "Oh, it's not my cup. It's Rowdy's. I try to keep him awake with coffee."

Brad stopped a mere moment, his eyes reflecting his amusement. He returned the cup to his lips and drained it. "Rowdy has good taste," he answered. His eyes ran over her body again. "In more ways than one."

Jo leaned back on the stall door. She studied the man before her, deciding that she liked him. There was nothing weak or apologetic about him. He had a style all his own. Jo liked untamed things—things that did what they wanted, despite what society tried to dictate. She had always delighted in the free will of animals. This was the first time she had found it in a man.

"You should be home in your own bed," she said softly. "I know what a heavy workload Doc left you."

Brad threw his head back and laughed. "Don't you think I can handle it?"

Jo brazenly let her eyes wander over his body. She studied the muscles under his polo shirt; she watched the tension seep into his abdomen as her eyes caressed it. She forced herself to move her glance down his jeans, tracing his wide thighs. She brought it back to his face. She knew he wasn't used to the brashness of her undignified stares. "You look strong enough to handle anything," she said, pleased with her nervy attitude.

Brad tossed his empty cup onto the cot. His expression had lost all sense of playfulness. His eyes filled with new emotion. He studied her carefully. Her hair draped around her shoulders like a halo. Her face had the look of an innocent nymph delighting in playful games. He tried to assess her. Was she just a tease, naive in the drive she could bring out in a man, or was she inviting him to take the next step? He watched her carefully, confused by the paradox between the fragile angel and the brazen woman. He watched, like a lion tracking his prey, and waited for her next move.

Jo's face broke into innocent amusement. She tilted her head and looked over at Rowdy "You're just lucky my guard dog hasn't had all his coffee. He'd handle you. Rowdy's pure terror when on duty."

She laughed lightly, obviously unaware of the seductive power she possessed. "You were smart to finish off his supply."

Brad forced a smile to his lips. *She is innocent,* he decided. *So innocent. This brazen little creature has a lot to learn about men, and I would like to be the one to teach her.*

Jo sat back down on the cot and patted the place next to her for him to sit. Brad refused her invitation. He picked up a large bale of straw as if it were a mere stalk and set it down a few feet in front of her. Jo watched in appreciation. It would take all her strength and several steps to lift it back to its spot. *I really need some strong help around this farm,* she mused. *Too bad I have to fire Mack.*

Brad spread his legs and sat down on the bale, one leg on each side. Jo liked the way he moved, with masculine power in socially unrestrained motion. She laughed. "I haven't seen anyone sit like that since I was a kid," she announced. She continued, closing her bright eyes, "Being raised on a trotting farm had its drawbacks. Horses that couldn't be ridden surrounded me, so I 'd saddle up a bale of straw. You know, put a fake head on it and blanket over the top. Then I'd pretend I was off on long runs through the fields. I'd bounce on the bale for hours." Her eyes mirrored her past thrill. "What fun," she sighed.

Brad studied her, amazed at her honesty. "Then what?" he asked intrigued.

She was enjoying sharing her story. Her eyes narrowed as if to remember the details in her mind. "Dad bought me the prettiest pony you ever saw. He was an appaloosa—white with chocolate spots." Her face glowed. "There was only one problem." Her eyes urged him to join the game by guessing.

"What?" Brad asked, totally fascinated with watching her.

"He was the meanest damn pony ever born. He threw me a dozen times. Once he even broke my leg—threw me over a fence," she laughed, as if delighted with the memory. "I swore I'd break that thing."

"Did you?" Brad asked, curious for the answer.

"Nope, Dad forbid me to ride him again. So I loved the dumb pony to death. You know, respected him for his own strength. We became best friends. He'd follow me everywhere like a big dog, dad used to say. I probably could have ridden him, but I didn't. I think people have to honor the pride of certain animals. You know, not break their spirit. Just love them for the way they are."

Brad became uneasy with her answer. "Not a very good philosophy for a horse trainer," he said seriously.

Jo felt the sting of his accusations, the hidden meaning being that she was just an emotional woman with no place in the serious business of the horse world. She leaned forward, her eyes growing large with feeling. "I'm a good horse trainer and a good manager," she said firmly. "I know what I have to do to train my horses. I just do it with love, not routine."

Brad smiled gently. He was impressed by her self-confidence. "I see," he answered simply. His eyes fell on the textbooks scattered around the cot. "Whose books are these?" he asked, picking one up in his hand.

Jo shifted her weight. "They're mine, from school. I was looking for an answer to Jupiter's injury."

Brad's eyes rose to meet hers. "So you think you need another opinion?"

Jo didn't apologize. "It's my horse, my decision. I was just checking out all my options."

Brad looked back down at the books. "Where did you go for your training?" he asked casually.

Jo moved her hand across the cot. She resented having to justify her experience to this man; Jo realized she should be quizzing his references. She was glad, however, to finally prove her own professionalism. "I went to SCAD in Georgia. I earned a B.A. in Equestrian Studies." She watched the surprise register across his face.

"Good school," he acknowledged. "I've known a few good trainers from that college."

Jo raised herself from the cot, grateful he realized just how good her training had been. "What about you?" she asked politely. "Old Doc said you come with good references."

Brad followed her movements. He watched her sway as she walked, her hair flowing behind her like silk. "I went to Texas A and M, like all good, southern boys who want to be vets."

Jo turned, leaning back against the pile of hay, casually digging the toe of her boot into the dirt floor to free a big stone. "I noticed your drawl," she said, stooping to pick up the rock. "Where are you from?"

Brad rose and crossed over to her. He stood close to her body, his hands grasping her shoulders. "Let's stop skirting around. I was raised on a horse farm just like you. I lived my life in Parrish, Kentucky, a small town not unlike this. After getting my degree, I went back to work on my uncle's horse farm. I'm here because old Doc is a friend of my uncle's. When he had a heart attack, my uncle called him up and suggested I could come help out. I'm good at everything I do. Just," his one hand reached up and touched her cheek, "as I'm sure you are."

Jo was taken off guard. She hadn't expected his forceful approach. She dropped the stone and her mouth flew open. Jo stared up into his eyes. His fingers felt hot against her cheek. "I see," she muttered, shaken. She moved away, suddenly uncomfortable around this powerful man. "Well, about Jupiter…"

Brad watched as she moved. She was like a skittish, young filly. "It's bad. One of the worst breaks I've ever seen. I could take X-rays. I could splint it. There are a number of things I could try. You know as well as I that they won't work. That horse will never be able to stand again. Why put it through such pain, such waste? Why run up bills for a needless cause?"

Jo turned around in anger. "It's not the money, I assure you. That horse will be worth a lot someday." The words caught in her throat. "He would have been."

Brad studied her. "Look," he said gently. "It's four a.m. You waited this long. Why don't we wait a few more hours and see what happens when the colt wakes up?"

Jo turned to stare at Jupiter. That's what we'll do," she said softly. "We'll wait until Jupiter wakes up." Jo could feel the panic setting in. If he didn't improve, it would be the end to her dreams and fantasies. "Thank you," she said softly; "thanks for coming over here."

Brad watched as she traced her finger along the stall door. Suddenly she looked very tired and sad. "I'm going to get a few winks of shuteye," he said. "Why don't you?"

Jo watched as he picked up another bale of hay and placed it end-to-end with the first. Then he lay his body down, tucking his hands behind his head for a pillow. "Sweet dreams," he mumbled as he closed his eyes.

Jo walked to her cot and lay down. She reminded herself of how often she had slept in the barn surrounded by animals. Somehow it was difficult with this animal man so close. *He's like a Clydesdale,* she reassured herself, as she closed her eyes. *A big, stud Clydesdale.*

She was at the track, ahead of all the other horses. Her hair was billowing behind her as she sat in the racing cart. Jo flipped her whip and urged the animal on, but this time it wasn't Jupiter; this time she was urging the Clydesdale male to victory.

Three

They woke together, Jupiter's painful whinny jarring them from their varied dreams. Jo was on her feet before she knew where she was or what had happened. Brad was beside her. She faltered, not yet steady in her surroundings. She felt his hands reach out and steady her. She shrugged him off, jerking away. "Let go of me; that's my horse in there," she yelled as she ran to Jupiter's stall.

Her hand shook as she slid the bar to open the stall door. Jupiter's eyes were wide with panic, his body trembling with sweat and fury. The colt was trying to get to his feet, trying to gain control over his own fate. His mouth curled back as he called out in long neighs of desperation. Jo threw her body against him, talking in slow, steady phrases. He looked at her, immediately reacting to her presence. He succumbed to her demands, lowering back down to the straw bed. Jo laid her body over his front quarter. "Atta boy, Jupiter," she crooned. "We're gonna take a look at what's hurting you. Breathe in, my boy. Just lay still."

Brad watched from the doorway. He'd seen love between horses and owners all his life, but this was something different. These two were bonded to each other with total trust and commitment. It was the only thing that could explain how a 100-pound woman could control 1400 pounds of terrified horse. He studied them as her hands roamed over her horse's neck, her lips whispering in Jupiter's ear. The horse's body stopped twitching and shaking, his eyes lost that look of terror and his head lay back down on the straw.

"You can come in now," Jo announced. "Please give him another shot before you touch his leg. I don't care how much it costs," she urged.

"Whatever you say, Jo," Brad said as he stepped into the stall. His tone reflected his newfound respect. Jupiter reacted to his presence. He raised his head, annoyed at the man's intrusion. Brad automatically called out to the horse; "It's all right, Jupiter."

Jupiter's eyes shot wide open; the horse lost focus on Jo and her soothing words. Raw panic and recurring pain took over. His head jerked up in a last ditch attempt to rear up. Brad heard the noise as it smacked into Jo and then forced her to slide down the horse's body. Brad reached out, catching her, preventing her from the flailing hoofs of the desperate animal. His hands encircled her rib cage under her breasts and he lifted her to her feet. "Jo, are you all right?" he asked as he spotted the wound on her cheek. It was bleeding and already changing colors. "You're hurt!" he called out alarmed.

"Let go of me," Jo ordered. "Give me a minute to get him settled down again. Don't talk. Just give him the shot and get my boy out of pain," she snarled. Her eyes looked as wild as her horse's. She turned and dove back on the rearing horse, talking to him in soothing tones. "Jupiter, it's me. Just the two of us, right? Come on, boy. I won't let anyone hurt you. Listen to me, Jupiter," she said and the horse refocused on his owner's voice. "Just lie down again. It's less painful. Just lie down, big boy," she said, her arms rubbing his neck again, her lips near his ear.

Jupiter's eyes calmed again. He was exhausted, still groggy from his first dose of pain medicine. He listened to her voice and within ten minutes was relaxed and calm. Brad quickly injected him with more pain medicine. He moved out of the stall and watched as the woman and her horse lay together, as Jupiter fell into another deep sleep.

Brad re-entered the stall and Jo moved slowly off her horse. She walked back toward his wounded leg and stooped down. Her fingers kneaded into Jupiter's leg, assessing her horse's injury. The attempts to stand on it had only made the swelling worse. Blood was seeping out through a cut where the broken bone was now exposed through the skin. Jo stood, walked past Brad, disheveled, bruised and heartsick. Without eye contact, she moved slowly toward the barn door. Brad knew she was headed toward her favorite place, the fence.

Forty-five minutes later, he found her there, sitting on the fence, staring up at the stars. She heard him walking up, felt his weight ease back down on the fence beside her. They sat for a few minutes with only the sounds of still night around them, owls whoed, frogs croaked, and crickets chirped.

"I promise you, Jo, if there were anything that could be done, I'd make sure Jupiter had that chance. I see how much you mean to each other," Brad stated.

"It always amazes me how quickly life can change," she admitted. "In less than ten minutes, everything turned ugly and painful."

Brad sat quietly, letting her words slip away into the black of the night. Finally, he suggested, "It's the work we do. We're tied to our horses. If all is well with them, life's good. Times like this are the hardest, almost unbearable."

"Almost," she said softly. "Do what needs to be done. I won't let him suffer anymore."

Jo laid her cheek next to Jupiter's soft skin and murmured into his ear, "I love you, Jupiter. I love you." Finally, she called out, "Brad, put my boy down."

Jo turned back to Jupiter. Wrapping her fingers around his thick mane, she used it to hold her as she slid down so she could hear his heartbeat. She pressed her ear against his warm body, loving the smell of this wonderful animal. She heard the thick, slow beat. It sounded strong, healthy. Tears slipped down her face onto her horse. She heard Brad filling the needle, and then he moved to make the injection. She lay there, listening as the big heart that had been dedicated to her slowly stopped beating. She remained there until she felt all the muscles in his body were still. Only then, did she let go of Jupiter's mane and slid off. He was gone.

"Do you have a knife on you?" she asked, as she wiped her tears away with the back of her arm.

"Yes, I do. He went to his bag and returned with a sharp scapula. He handed it to her, without questioning her intent. "Thanks," she said with a slight shrug. Jo climbed back on her dead horse. She sat on top, by his neck, and carefully removed Jupiter's mane. Then she slid off, wiped the knife on her jeans and handed it back. He watched her walk out of the stall swinging Jupiter's mane.

Jo felt angry—angry at the world. Silently, she made a vow; *I will not crumble in defeat. No matter what, I will prove out my horses. Fate will not take victory away from me again.*

Jo strode over to the small filly's stall. Little Girl walked over to greet her. She pushed her soft nose against Jo's palm searching for a treat. Jo studied her carefully. "You're such a small filly," she said softly.

Jo reached up and tied Jupiter's mane to one of the bars in Little Girl's stall saying, "It's all we have left of your brother." Little Girl watched her, the nostrils twitching with the new scent. Then, the filly turned and began walking around the ring she had created in her stall. "No wonder you're so darn skinny and small," Jo said.

Jo took a few deep breaths. She thought of how surprisingly fast Little Girl had occasionally been. Jo had been forced to hold her back, afraid she would hurt herself, but the horse was a stall walker. All night she roamed around her stall, restless and searching. She'd even worn a track in the meadow where she grazed, constantly walking. She seemed to be searching for something.

Jo heard Brad approach and turned toward him, saying, "Meet Little Girl, Jupiter's sister." She opened the door to the stall.

Brad watched as Jo slid her hands up Little Girl's legs, like a buyer examining a possible investment. He could see the determination growing in Jo's eyes. "She's very thin and skittish," he said, almost unwillingly.

"I'll work on that," Jo said, commitment in her voice. "You'd be surprised how fast she is, Brad. Everyone might be." Her eyes looked up into his. There was renewed life there and undaunted spirit.

Brad smiled and shook his head. "Good luck."

Mack entered the barn. He swaggered in with his usual teenage gait. "What's up, Jo?" he asked as he spotted the cot and bales of straw. He turned to focus his blank look on Brad.

Jo walked away from Little Girl. She closed the stall door, feeling it necessary to protect the horse from the carelessness of the confused boy. As she did, Jupiter's mane swung past her. It ignited a fury she had been holding down. She wanted to beat the boy, hit him with anything close at hand. She breathed in, slowing her rage and taking back control of her emotions. Still, when she turned, Jo's eyes reflected her outrage. "Jupiter's dead. A broken leg from being left in the west paddock next to the mares," she screamed. She watched as the boy tried to grasp everything that she had said. He fidgeted around, shifting his adolescent weight.

"I can't believe it," he stammered. "I thought he'd be okay. The guys came around. Billy got a new car; I never thought. I can't believe....." He searched for an answer, his hands moving in the air, looking for the right words to excuse his actions.

Jo was too tired for any further drama. She pointed at him saying, "You're fired, Mack. Just get out of here and leave me alone." Jo walked over to the barn phone. It hung on the wall next to the tack room, representing her dreams of a future office. She looked up the number for carcass removal and made the call. "Mr. Ream? This is Jo Martin, out in rural delivery seven. You know, Hobby Horse Farm. Can you come out and pick up a dead horse this morning? I want him out by noon." Jo hung up.

Brad was standing there, listening and watching. "I see you got a new bag," Jo said, motioning to the case he held in his hand. "Wait a moment," she suggested, as she bent down to examine it. "That's old Doc's bag. I can see a few of Rowdy's teeth marks on it." She looked up at him from her position on the floor. Her face had a slight smile and her eyes seemed bright again. Brad was taken back by her power to renew herself and survive.

"That's right," he answered simply. "I'll keep it up from now on."

Jo rose from her inspection. "Where's Rowdy?" she asked casually. She walked out the barn doors, not stopping to again mourn the dead colt.

Rowdy was busy with Brad's tires. He was circling the jeep, marking each one. Jo threw her head back and laughed. "Hey, Brad. You're a marked man."

Brad watched her as the sunlight hit her hair. He listened as her laughter floated to him. Somehow, he already knew he was marked, perhaps for life.

Brad moved out into the sunlight next to her. He laid a finger gently on her cheek. It was badly bruised and still bleeding. A large black and blue mark was already forming on the swelled area under her eye. "You're hurt, Jo," he said, concerned. "Better let me check it."

Jo looked up into his eyes. "Why Brad, whateveryourname, you're just a horse doctor. You can't fix people."

Brad smiled and backed away, "You're right; I never told you my full name. It's Brad Kirby. Nice to meet you, by the way."

Jo extended her hand, "Nice to meet you. You've been a good friend. Thanks."

Brad noticed how small her hand was compared to his. He also noticed her calluses and thought, *She's been spending hours in carts training her horses.* Brad leaned toward her and said, "I'll spend the night with you anytime,"

Jo felt the message flow through her like a sip of strong whiskey. It warmed her and sent a glow up her spine. "I'll remember that," she said laughing.

Brad watched her carefully. "You'll need some new help. You can't handle all the work around here with just Ruben. Can I send over one of the extra hands from a larger farm?"

Jo lifted her chin high and stared at him. "No, thanks. We'll be all right. Do me a favor though," she said earnestly. "Don't tell too many people about what happened. It might cause trouble with the owners of the mares I stable here. I need those monthly payments. My reputation can't be doubted." Her heart skipped a beat; she was fighting for her farm.

Brad smiled saying, "Don't worry, Jo. It's nobody's business. It wasn't your fault. I should have known that from the beginning." He saw the relief come over her face and added, "No SCAD graduate would put a colt next to mares."

Jo smiled, flinching as she felt the pain it caused in her cheek. "You're an okay guy for a stranger."

Brad laughed. "One minute I'm your friend, the next I'm a stranger. What's next, Jo?"

Jo raised her hand and touched his lips with her fingertips. "Who knows, Doc, who knows?" She watched as his face reflected his interest. His lips parted and pulled one fingertip between them. His front teeth closed gently on her finger while his tongue licked across the tip twice. Then, he released it and smiled. Jo felt the heat rise to her face, the beat of her heart skip. She lowered her hand slowly.

"You taste of horses and nectar," he said slowly. "A different combination."

Jo stood motionless as Brad strolled to his jeep. He moved with a steady gait, one meant for the long journey, not the short victory. Jo put her hands on her hips. *He might not be a Clydesdale after all,* she mused. *He might be another appaloosa. Another untamable pony whose gonna throw me over and hurt me.*

Jo turned away as the jeep pulled out of the drive. She turned her attention back to the farm. *The mares have to be fed, the filly has to be let out and trained, and the stall Jupiter died in must be cleaned up and freshened. Life must go on,"* Jo thought quietly—no matter how hard it is.

The next few days slipped by in a maze of activity. Jo worked from morning to nightfall, overseeing the details of the farm. She was determined that no oversights would ever harm her animals again. She hauled in the feed, straining her back under fifty-pound sacks; she swept out the barn, making sure it was a showplace of cleanliness and organization; she checked each mare, watching for briar or insect bites; and spent at least three hours working with Little Girl, trying everything to bring the small filly around. At the completion of each task, she found herself thinking that Brad would be impressed, that he would appreciate all she had accomplished.

The days began to take their toll. Jo was tired and her muscles ached. Every job grew harder, as her body seemed to call out for sleep. Sound sleep, however, was impossible. Jo now slept on a cot in the stall next to Little Girl. She was determined to stop the filly's stall-walking. Her sleep came in small patches, since the nights were filled with sporadic trips to Little Girl's side. She would stroke the filly's head, reassuring, calming down, and urging her to sleep. Little Girl reacted favorably. Her nightly trips around the stall slowed down, and her large eyes closed for occasional snatches of light sleep. The horse began to gain some weight, unlike her owner. Each pound Little Girl gained, Jo seemed to lose. She gave her energy to her horse, and as long as the arrangement was working for the filly, Jo was willing to go on.

It had been a week since Brad's late-night visit. During the first few days, Jo had caught herself looking at the driveway, hoping to see the arrival of his jeep. She had dressed with extra care, making sure she was clean and attractively attired. He never came. She had daydreamed he would arrive as she was training Little Girl. She had hoped he would stand at the training track and watch as Little Girl's legs picked up speed and strength. He never came. She brushed her filly's chestnut coat until it shone under the sunlight in highlights of fiery red and black. He never appeared to see her efforts. Finally, at the end of the first week, Jo forced Brad from her mind. She decided his interest had been nothing more than a causal flirtation. Little Girl became the only living thing that promised possible reward.

The sunlight was fading as Jo walked into the barn. She was dressed in just a terry bathrobe, pulled over her body after her shower. She'd thought of one more job to be done. It had been a very hot day, and she realized the water troughs must have been used heavily. While her roast cooked in the oven, Jo left to refill them. As she finished pouring water into the stallion's trough, she stopped to check him over. He was a mighty beast, and she stroked him tenderly. She left and filled her bucket again. It seemed heavier after the day's hard work. Her arms ached. She started toward Little Girl's stall and stropped halfway. She sat, for just a moment, to rest on the open cot beside the stall. She was too tired, so weary. Jo lay down, thinking, *just five minutes*. Her legs felt like lead as she raised them from the floor and placed them on the cot. Her eyes closed and she thought, *maybe ten minutes of sleep—a short nap.* Jo fell into a sound sleep, her one hand still holding the handle of the water bucket. The sun set, letting the barn fill with deep, peaceful dark. Jo's body claimed what it needed, rest.

Brad had forced himself to stay away from the farm. He told himself that he had his own work to do—his own worries with horses, some valued at over three million dollars. He couldn't become involved with pipe dreams for a filly with short legs and poor breeding. He scolded himself, reasoning *I'm a vet, trained to be objective and analytical.* Still, thoughts of the golden-haired nymph pulled at his subconscious. The whispered oath of love to her horse touched his heart. During the week, he had watched as rich, well-heeled owners came in their Cadillac Escalades or BMW's to make their token visits to the barns. Brad thought of Jo, working herself to the bone over her animals. As sophisticated women, dressed in high heels and linen suits, came to see their spouse's horses, Brad thought of Jo, in her faded jeans, sleeping in the barn with crazy Rowdy under her cot. She began to fill his thoughts more each day, and he decided the separation wasn't working. Perhaps he was making more out of his brief contact with the woman than he should. He pulled his jeep into her driveway. He had to check to see if his impression was correct, if she really existed as he had come to envision her.

Brad knocked on the back door of the farmhouse. No answer came. He looked around the fields and toward the barn; no lights were on. *She has to be inside the house,* he reasoned. He had come this far and suddenly he was desperate to see her, so much so that he boldly opened the door and walked inside.

The house was filled with the warming aroma of supper cooking. He called out her name, "Jo?" Anyone home?" he snapped on some lights, amazed at the comfortable feeling the room evoked.

He smiled to himself. The house was decorated just as he would have imagined. The walls were covered with neatly framed horse pictures; the fireplace mantel held family portraits. Brad walked toward the mantel, drawn by a picture of Jo and her mother. Carefully, he picked it up. Jo was just a little girl, her eyes bigger than they should be, her face as innocent as it was in his thoughts. The woman beside her was beautiful, a mirror of Jo now, but taller and larger in build. Brad placed the portrait back on the mantel. He moved into the kitchen.

It was a typical farmhouse kitchen, a large table sitting in the center of the room, plants hanging in all the windows. Brad smiled, as she spotted a bright yellow canary dozing lazily in a wicker cage. *This woman*, he mused, *seems to surround herself with living things to love.*

It was just a farmhouse kitchen, but it felt good, smelled glorious. It made him feel like staying for supper and talking around the old, oak table. He opened the oven door and used two hand-woven potholders to pull out the roast. It was overcooked, starting to burn. For the first time, Brad worried. Flashes of tiny Jo among the huge animals made shivers run up his spine. Thoughts of how she had so easily bruised with Jupiter's quick, clumsy movement made images appear. He sat the roast on a potholder on the counter and walked through the house, calling her name.

The bedroom was fresh and clean, just her tee shirt, panties and jeans on the bed. Her boots stood beside it. Brad's worry increased. Jo didn't seem the type to go anywhere without her boots. He moved quickly, now overcome with fear.

He walked out the front door and headed toward the barn. He couldn't image Jo anywhere but on the farm. She seemed rooted to the place. He heard Rowdy growl as he came in the barn door and felt his heartbeat quicken. Brad flipped on the lights and scanned the scene. His eyes fell on Jo, sound asleep in just her white robe, her hair falling over the sides of the cot like a golden waterfall, her small hand clutching the handle of the pail. Relieved, he breathed in, and then his breath caught in his throat.

She looked beautiful and very thin, a large patch of fading black and blue still on her cheek. Brad moved over to the cot, careful not to wake her. As he stared down at her, a protective drive stirred within him. Gently, he reached down and lifted her into his arms. She mumbled softly and cuddled her head against his chest. *Like a rag doll,* he thought as he carried her toward the house. Her soft hair fell against his cheek, tantalizing him with the arousing aroma of soap and fresh air. His breath came harder, not from exertion, but rather from the nearness of the woman in his arms. He could sense the rise of her firm breasts against his chest, a mere robe hiding her body from his view. He had been wrong to come. He cursed himself as he carried Jo through the darkness toward her house. *This woman is too captivating, too compelling,*" he warned himself. He entered the house and walked toward Jo's bedroom. He stopped for a minute, regretting having to let her go, but slowly he lowered Jo onto the double bed.

Jo moaned in appreciation of its softness. He lifted the covers and moved her bare feet under them. *Tiny feet* he thought, *little toes.* She slid under the sheets, the robe opening slightly to expose her legs. *Beautiful,* Brad thought, *thin and shapely.* He forced himself to pull the covers over her body, tucking them around her chin. She opened her eyes, sleep still hazing the deep brown pools. "Brad! How nice," she whispered, still half asleep. Her arms reached up without hesitation. They encircled his neck, urging him toward her. Her lips gently kissed his, a natural show of giving, so much a part of Jo. She smiled and rolled over, releasing him from her grasp.

Jo fell asleep, the first sound sleep since Jupiter's death. Something told her she could rest. Her subconscious knew Brad was there, and he would take over while she slept.

Brad stared down at the woman, tenderness filling him. He had felt her trust and confidence. He had sensed her transmittal of responsibility. Somehow he knew she slept because he was there.

Brad walked out of the room and away from the house, heading toward the barn. He filled Little Girl's water trough, then decided to check the filly over. He studied her, amazed at how she had increased in weight. Then he stepped forward and felt her legs, assessing the muscles and appraising her worth. She was a strong filly, stronger than he had originally thought. He smiled. It was obvious how much work Jo had done with her.

His eyes roamed around the clean barn. Jo was everywhere. He could see her loving touches and her attention to details. She had braided Jupiter's mane and hung it next to a snapshot of the horse on a wall by her phone. It brought back memories of the fateful night they had shared. He decided she was as remarkable as he had hoped.

Brad folded the cot and moved it to the side, thinking *she can't go on like this*. He walked back to the farmhouse, eager to be closer to the woman he so admired.

Brad settled on the sofa. It was comfortable. The coffee table was covered with horse magazines. He flipped through them. Jo had scribbled a notation next to an article describing a new procedure for deworming horses. His lips curled into a slight grin. She had written, *show Brad*.

Jo dreamed she was riding her appaloosa pony. He was bigger now, with strong thighs and firm legs. She rode on his back, the wind blowing her hair around in swirls keeping her from seeing clearly. She felt the strength of the animal beneath her. They moved in unison, her pelvis rubbing across his strong body. They moved faster and faster, increasing their pace. Their motion became rhythmic patterns, her hips rolling forward and then back. The appaloosa carried her along until she lost total control, then reared onto his back legs and clawed at the wind with his front hoofs. He raised his head and neighed his warning with fury. He didn't want to be broken—to be ridden. She felt herself falling from his back. She couldn't see the obstacles ahead, but she could sense the coming pain. Suddenly she was viciously thrown aside, left to fall, until she saw the fence. Jo screamed, "No! No! Not again."

Brad was at her side in seconds. He took her into his arms and rocked her back and forth. She was confused, lost between two worlds. She reached around him, pulling him closer, holding on lest she keep falling. She dug her nails into his flesh, afraid to let go.

"Jo," he whispered softly "It's all right, I'm here.

Jo raised her head slowly. She searched through her misty, confused world for his eyes, as if they were the answer to the puzzle. She found them, deep pools of concern. "Brad, where am I?" she asked, her confusion still not satisfied.

"You're in my arms, digging your nails into my back," he said softly, his face gentle with tenderness.

Jo released her hold. She ran a hand over her face, trying to wash off the sleep. "What happened? How did I get here?" she asked, her eyes darting around her bedroom.

Brad rose to his feet, giving her the room her spirit demanded. "I brought you in from the barn. Good lord, Jo, you can't go on working yourself to death." His eyes carried no message of recrimination, just concern.

Jo smiled up at him like sunlight breaking though the storm. "It looks good, doesn't it? The barn, I mean."

He laughed at her open pride. "Yes, it does and so does the filly. She's improving. I checked her over."

Jo's eyes lit up with happiness. She pulled her knees up to her chin, her hands encircling both the covers and her legs. "She's getting faster too, Brad. I found the secret. I spend my nights in the barn with her. Then I can keep her stall-walking down to a minimum. I think she's just lonely."

"You mean you've been sleeping in the barn every night?"

Jo bristled at his tone. "Why, yes. She needs me."

Brad realized that he had to be careful not to overreact to her dedication. He decided to change the subject. "How long has it been since you've eaten a good meal?"

"Jo's body went into immediate motion as her brain registered her mistake. She leaped from her bed, tugging absently at the robe around her. "I put a pot roast in. I planned to bulk up with protein tonight," she called back as she ran toward the kitchen. "It must be burnt to a crisp. What time is it anyhow?"

"I took it out," he yelled after her, laughing at her ability to heal her own holes of energy.

Jo stood barefoot in the kitchen, her fingers picking at the roast while she nibbled on the scraps they pulled off. "You saved it. It's still edible. How about a big, roast beef sandwich?" Jo felt happy again. Brad had come! He did care. He was her friend.

"Sounds great," Brad answered, pulling out a chair from the table. He watched as Jo scurried around the kitchen. She chatted on about how well Little Girl was doing. She pointed out her canary and showed her delight when it broke into a soft song. It had been so long since anyone had come into her house and sat with her in the kitchen. It was enjoyable to chat with someone who shared her love for horses and understood her lifestyle. The kitchen felt friendlier, homey and happy. Jo envisioned how Little Girl must feel when she stayed with her. She could now understand how lonely the horse had been. Jo equated everything in her life to horses, even her own emotions.

Brad sat, joining in her chatter. He told her about the horses at the other farms. They laughed over the rich owners' spouses coming to the barns in high heels.

"Next time," Jo said, laying a sandwich in front of him, "Pick up a shovel full of manure, and ask the woman to hold it a minute while you get a wheelbarrow." Brad joined in; her quick sense of humor was infectious.

They sat for hours, drinking beer, eating several beef sandwiches and talking. Jo dashed from the room, carrying back the article for Brad to read. He politely read through it, delighting in her interest in his work.

The grandfather clock rang out one chime. Brad realized he was keeping her from what she most needed, sleep. "You, my friend," he said, rising from his chair, "must get more rest." He carried their plates over to the sink. "I'll do the dishes before I leave."

Jo watched as he moved around in her kitchen. She relished his company, enjoyed their companionship. She wasn't ready to have him leave. She felt like Little Girl, afraid to be alone lest she roam around her house throughout the night. Jo walked over to his side, "Brad, don't go."

Her words evoked desire in him. He forced himself to wait, not to jump to conclusions. "What do you want, Jo?" he asked, his voice deep and noncommittal.

"I want you to just hold me," she said, as she wrapped her arms around his waist. She hugged his body close to her, nuzzling her head against his chest.

Brad picked her up in his arms and carried her to the bedroom, turning off the lights as he went. He laid her on the bed, his mind concentrating on keeping his desire under control.

Jo relaxed and suddenly her entire body seemed to melt into the mattress. She craved sleep. "Let's cuddle," she suggested, too tired to care what he might think of her.

Brad took off his boots and unbuttoned his shirt. His chest was covered with thick, blonde hair. *The color of rich honey,*" she thought watching through sleepy nods. He hesitated at his jeans, still unsure of what she wanted. He watched as she fought off sleep, decided to wait, and came to the bed with them on. She curled up into his arms, resting her head against his bare chest. He could feel her breath, softly blowing against his skin. He held her close to him, closing his eyes, waiting for her next move.

Jo pushed against him. He was warm and his scent was intoxicating. Her lips kissed the skin over his heart and she cuddled closer, moving her hips next to his. She draped a leg over his thigh, a subconscious movement so he couldn't get away. She felt protected and succumbed to deep sleep.

The canary stopped singing; the house quieted. Only the tick of a grandfather clock and the beat of Brad's heart could be heard. Jo slept, locked in his arms, her warm body draped over his. He lay very still, afraid to move. He felt as though he was holding an angel in his arms, and he didn't want her to fly away. He forced himself to settle for her closeness. He knew he could have her, but tonight was not the night. He would wait. He wanted her awake and strong when he took her and made her his.

Five

Jo reached over in bed, looking for Brad's warmth. He was gone. She opened her eyes and scanned the bedroom. He'd left.

Jo rolled over on her back and stretched. It'd been a long time since she'd felt the nearness of a man beside her, five long years. A small smile curved her lips as she inhaled deeply. The room still held his body's aroma and a hint of his lime aftershave. Her knowledge of breeding made Jo realize that her brain was being enticed by the pheromones that Brad's body had left on her sheets. Jo ran her fingers through her long hair, dragging a strand from across her nose. Even it held his scent and a shiver ran through her. *He's all man*, she thought, remembering his body against hers. She shook her head, eager to erase the memory, yet knowing it was useless. He'd invaded every corner of her private life: her barn, her kitchen, and her bedroom. He was everywhere, even in her dreams.

Jo laid her hands over her face, thinking *He's going to leave. He's going to hurt me.* A sad smile crossed her lips. *I've been hurt before. I've learned to bounce back,* her thoughts continued. *The emotional ride might be worth the fall, just as long as I prepare for the pain.*

Jo's deliberation returned to Brad. She closed her eyes and pictured him at her kitchen table. She remembered his deep, warm voice filling the room with his presence. She wrapped her arms around herself, trying to evoke the feeling of comfort he'd given throughout the night. Finally, her eyes opened wide.

I can't do this! I can't let him become the primary interest in my life. Her chin jetted up and she threw the blankets aside. *I have to think of the work ahead of me. Little Girl and I have so much to accomplish. I can't let him invade my life.*

Jo jumped out of bed, walking with determination toward the bathroom. She was eager to wash all traces of him away. Jo Martin was bent on preparing for the fall, the hurt. She was good at losing; she'd done it so often. She didn't realize that she didn't know how to win. Jo had never been allowed to taste true victory. As a result, she'd begun to train for the loss, braced for the fall. Jo hadn't acquired a winner's heart; she'd only developed the stiff, upper lip of a good loser.

Jo wrapped the filly's legs in cotton pads and ace bandages, the last step before the track. Once there, Jo knew she'd have no time to think of Brad. Little Girl was skittish; she'd stall-walked all night. Jo regretted putting her own needs over the filly's and apologized saying, "It won't happen again, I promise." Jo pulled her toward the ring, intent on building Little Girl's stamina in time for the fair.

She picked up a bag of barbecue chips as she passed the tack room. She'd overslept and left no time for breakfast. Jo was starving. She ripped the bag open with her teeth. Then, holding it in the hand that was tugging Little Girl, she grabbed a bunch with her free one. Jo walked slowly toward the track, thinking and munching. She jumped when she felt Little Girl's soft nose nudging at the bag. Jo smiled to herself and stopped. "Little Girl, don't tell me you want potato chips?" She dug into the bag and pulled out a handful. The filly ate them down, grabbing them with her soft lips. Jo laughed. "So I found your passion—Utz potato chips." She offered the horse another handful. "If you want a snack of barbecue chips, that's fine with me," Jo said, smiling. "Just earn them." Jo led the horse to the track, saving the rest of the chips till after the session.

Rowdy passed them, another bullfrog in his mouth. Jo just shook her head and smiled. "I guess we all have our weaknesses," she said softly, thinking of Brad. "Let's just keep them under control," she continued, more to herself.

Jo had increased the filly's training schedule. She knew the horse had to build up speed and stamina, yet she was afraid. Little Girl was still tired, still skinny. She hitched up the training cart and settled into the seat. Jo raised her feet up, putting her heels in the metal stirrups. It was an uncomfortable position, but Jo was used to it. She'd driven pacers since she was fifteen years old. Taking the reins in her hands, she headed Little Girl around the ring, keeping the horse in a slow, even jog. The dust and dirt blew up around her; the wheels hummed under her, reflecting the speed. Jo was at work and here Brad couldn't enter her mind. Here it was just the horse and the woman, out to improve their speed, out to improve their track record.

They always jogged the wrong way around the track. *It isn't time to turn her yet*, Jo thought. Only when a horse had built up the leg muscles to gain good speed would they be turned the racing way. The horses were never jogged in the direction of the race; that was saved for the fast pace of top speed. That was the final step in training, the final signal for the horse to go for the win. Jo wasn't sure Little Girl was ready, so despite the short amount of time left before the race, Jo kept the horse jogging the wrong way. It never dawned on Jo that she was the one not ready to race.

They went around the track for four miles, the hot August sun beating down on both of them. Jo pulled her to the side and hopped off the seat. She stroked the horse gently, checking her for injuries.

Jo led the filly to the adjoining paddock and pumped the well for water. She filled the bucket and washed the horse down, scraping off excess moisture with the sweat-trough. Then she led her filly to the barn to unwrap the horse's legs and give her the promised treat. Little Girl devoured the rest of the chips, nudging Jo for more. "Sorry, girl, you've eaten them all," Jo announced, brushing off her hands. "I'll go to the factory and buy you your own supply," she bargained, "if you continue to work for me." Jo patted the horse gently on the head. "I'll do anything, Little Girl, to help you gain weight and settle down."

Just then, a truck pulled into her drive. She knew Ruben was in the front, hitching the drag on the back of the tractor so he could smooth the dirt track after the morning workout. He could see what it was. Jo turned back to her chores. She unwrapped Little Girl's legs and walked her back out to her private paddock. She returned to muck out three stalls. She picked up the pitchfork and dragged the cart over to the stallion's stall. This was Jo's least favorite job, cleaning up after the animals she cared for. The horseflies flew around her face as she began loading up the hay and manure. It was mere manual labor, but it was too much for Ruben. She worried about his health. He'd looked so tired lately, almost as though the death of Jupiter had affected his will to go on. *I have to get his spirits up,* she decided. Jo felt responsible to oversee everything on her farm. She wondered what delivery the unknown truck in her drive was making. She hadn't ordered anything that she could remember.

Ruben came to the barn door, confusion on his face. "Jo," he called out, "better get out here."

Jo dropped the pitchfork and brushed off her hands. Rowdy picked up a dried flake of manure and began tossing it around in the air. "Stop that, Rowdy," she warned, throwing an old apple core at him. "You'll get that mess all over the barn floor." Rowdy ran outside with his treasure, growling in play. "Jo sighed, thinking, *what a dumb dog.*

On her way out of the barn, she stopped to check a mousetrap. It held a squashed mouse. She picked the trap up and carried it with her out the door.

Rowdy had dropped his treasure and was busy smelling the tires of the old truck in the drive. Jo didn't recognize it. She walked over, still holding the trap. Noises came from the rear, so she headed toward the truck's back. Her steps halted as she caught sight of Brad. He was dressed in a green tee shirt and jeans. The green made his honey-colored hair seem richer, thicker. His face was set in determination as he tugged on something inside the truck. His arm muscles were flexed in his work, forming waves under the tanned skin. *He's so handsome,* Jo noted. She felt her breath leave her, her palms become moist. Those arms had held her throughout the night. That body had given its warmth to her. Now she knew she wanted more of him; she longed to explore every inch of the man. She ached to go over and touch him, to feel his tanned skin. She remembered how delightfully their bodies had fit together, how firm his stomach had been beside her. She suddenly recalled the virility she'd felt within him. She'd been so tired that she hadn't thought of it before. Somewhere in her dream she recalled feeling the man come alive, feeling his body react to their closeness. Jo pushed her hair back with her hand. She was amazed that she could have just slept beside the magnificent specimen before her.

Brad's eyes lifted from the truck and caught her stare. Her face reflected her interest. In her hands she held the mousetrap, like most women hold their purses. The dead mouse hung, dangling in the air by its back leg. He laughed and asked, "Do you carry dead mice everywhere you go?"

Her face warmed under his stare. "Isn't it ridiculous?" she commented, as she opened the trap and picked the dead mouse out. "Have you ever heard of a barn using traps to catch rodents?" Her eyes danced in the sunlight. "It's Rowdy, you know. He hates cats. He chases them off, then refuses to kill anything but bullfrogs. What a waste he is." She walked over to a garbage can and dumped in the mouse. Then she crossed over to the truck. "What in the world have you got there?"

"If I can ever get it out, it's the answer to your sleepless nights," he answered, again straining at the object in the truck. Ruben returned to his work. He started the tractor and headed toward the track.

Jo moved closer to Brad. As she came around the truck, her eyes opened wide. "A goat?" she laughed, lightly. "You brought me a goat?"

Brad gave one more tug and hauled the struggling animal out. "You bet," he said, happily steadying the animal with his hands.

It was the dumbest looking goat Jo had ever seen, thin and spindly. It began nibbling on her jeans and then raised its head nudging her hands, no doubt smelling the potato chips. "Just what I need to win races," she sighed, "a scrawny goat."

Brad's eyes looked down into hers. She could feel their splash of blue sweep over her, like a refreshing spray of cold water. They sent a chill through her body, and she forced herself not to quiver visibly "This, my dear friend," he said slowly, the words sounding intimate after last night, "is the answer to Little Girl's stall-walking. She's just lonely." He lifted a hand to cup Jo's chin. "She needs a little attention to make her settle down."

Jo felt his fingers against her skin. Unable to contain her reaction, she quivered at his touch. Her eyes lifted to look into his. He'd felt the movement, and a slow smile spread across his face. "Well, you've just restored my self-confidence," he whispered "I've never taken a woman to bed to have her fall asleep in my arms. You damaged my ego."

Jo met his stare honesty. "There are two sides of you, Brad. One is my friend, always there when I need you and the other...." Jo's eyes dropped from his face.

Brad's hand slid around her waist, "The other?" he inquired.

"The other is a side I don't know, but I'm beginning to suspect it's one I wouldn't have felt safe with last night."

Brad asked, "Is that what you want, safety?" His hands lifted to her neck, his fingers moving gently. They traveled down her throat, taking her breath with them. The tips came under the collar of her blouse, invading her privacy, making her want them to move deeper under the fabric.

"You bring me no flowers, no candy," she said, fighting to keep control, "you bring me a flea-bitten goat and then hint of lust." His hands kept moving, back up her neck toward her ears. She closed her eyes and gave in to the wave of emotion he aroused. "You're as crazy as Rowdy, Brad," she whispered hoarsely.

He stepped closed to her, his breath coming against her skin. "I don't want to sleep under your cot. I don't want anything between us, especially not that damn terrycloth robe you wore last night."

Jo opened her eyes and searched his. She was foggy from emotions long ago suppressed. The revival made her dizzy, and she wondered, "*How could I have missed the pleasure and thrill of sex?*

"What do you want, Brad?" she whispered, an invitation for him to come closer, to touch more of her.

He stepped back, removing his hand. "Right now, all I want is to put this damn goat in with Little Girl," he declared, and then he smiled gently adding, "Later I want something very different."

Brad helped Jo clean up Little Girl's stall. The goat roamed around the barn, nibbling on everything it could reach. Rowdy chased after it, growling and nipping at its heels. Finally the goat had taken enough. It put its head down and pushed Rowdy away. Rowdy turned on his bowlegs and left the barn in a huff. He'd lost the battle. Jo laughed, "Now if that thing can catch mice, it's got a job."

Brad was busily spreading clean hay around Little Girl's stall. "It won't catch mice, but it might settle down your flighty filly. Just keep at least three inches of hay in the stall. It will be better for Little Girl's legs, and maybe it will tempt her to lie down." His eyes rose to meet hers. "Who knows, she may just want to cuddle." His lips curved into a smile.

"Who knows?" Jo teased back. "That's all the old goat is good for, isn't it?"

Brad grabbed her free arm and gently pulled her into the stall. He closed the door and lay down on the straw, his arms reaching up for her, inviting her to join him. She lay down beside him. He leaned over and caressed her hair. "I'm no old goat, Jo." His voice came in hoarse whispers. "I'm only thirty years old and full of more potential than just holding you." His hand reached beneath her shirt, and his fingers began kneading up her stomach toward her bare breasts. He moaned when he felt her naked skin. "No bra?" he questioned, as his fingertips ran over her erect nipples.

Jo moaned and turned toward him. She felt his power come to life; it made her body shake with desire. "I don't believe in restraints," she whispered. He withdrew his hand and lowered his mouth to hers, covering her lips with his strong kisses. She encircled her arms around him, urging him to lie on top of her. He did, the weight of his body pushing the urgency of his need next to her. She moaned his name, "Brad."

The sound of the tractor making its way back from the ring shocked both of them back to reality. "I want to taste you all over, horses and syrup," he whispered in her ear. His mouth moved from hers, running down her neck, tasting her skin as it roamed. Then he slowly stopped, raising himself carefully. Inch-by-inch he pulled away from her, so slowly that she hardly knew when all his weight was off her body. He stood, looking down at her. Her eyes were hazed with desire, her lips parted, inviting him to return. It took all his strength to hold back. "I want you, but I want to take you slowly. I want to taste you, and experience you inch by tender inch."

Jo heard the tractor coming closer, knew she should move. She didn't. He aroused her beyond all common sense. He stirred within her intense need and cravings. She'd experienced sex before, but it had been when she was still in college. Back then she'd been more thrilled with the promise of a pairing and a family. The boy had alluded to these things, as he satisfied only his own sexual needs. He'd been clumsy and awkward, leaving Jo with a dim view of lovemaking. He'd been just as unconcerned with her feelings when he didn't share her dream for their future, leaving her bitter and uninterested in any further relationships.

In contrast Brad was confident and experienced. No wonder she'd been able to live so long without a man's touch. She'd never really felt it before. Suddenly Jo knew she could not turn away from the needs Brad exposed within her, the hunger he aroused. She forced herself to sit up and deal with her raw feelings. Her lips curved into a forced smile, her hands began shaking. She lowered her eyes from his, fighting for self-control.

Jo straightened her blouse as Brad walked out of the barn. He would keep Ruben busy until she gathered her wits. She grabbed Little Girl's lead and walked out the back door toward the pasture where Little Girl was grazing. When she returned Brad had already put the goat in the stall. She smiled at him asking, "How should we introduce them to each other?"

Brad answered, "Just lead her in. We'll let nature take its course."

They stood outside the stall watching the animals as they sniffed each other in curiosity. Brad walked behind Jo and placed his arm on her shoulder. She felt his hands squeeze her arm and she closed her eyes. "Don't tease me," she asked. "I'm not sure I can handle it right now."

He pulled her closer to his side, their bodies touching and his hand caressed her golden hair "I promise, Jo. I will never leave you unsatisfied again."

Jo reached up and kissed his soft lips tenderly. She withdrew and placed her forehead on his chest. "It's my turn now, Brad."

She looked back up, into his eyes. "You can spend the night with me any time."

Brad looked into her deep, brown eyes. She gave so openly. She reacted too honestly; no ploys, no games. She invited him to take her. She asked for no promises. Brad lifted one hand and cupped her breast through the blouse. Then he turned and walked out of the barn. Brad had to think; this woman was too intoxicating. The more he saw her, the more he wanted her. He was suddenly afraid that when he did experience her total giving, he would never be able to leave her alone. Brad started the truck and drove out the drive. He had to think carefully, and he couldn't think when he was with Jo.

Six

The day passed slowly, an eternity filled with dragging sixty-second minutes. Jo wanted the day's work to be over, Ruben to leave the farm and Brad to come back to her. Six long hours, however, loomed before her. In an attempt to fill the time, she walked through the pasture toward the back acreage, one hand holding a bucket of nails, the other her hammer.

Jo needed to fence in a new section for the foals that would be born in the spring. The posthole digger and crew had already put in the posts. She'd planned to have Mack hang the fencing, but now it was up to her. The wire lay in a heavy roll in the field, a constant reminder of the never-ending work that surrounded her. Jo unrolled it, straining against its weight. She held it up to a post and began her task. It felt good to drive the nails into the wood; it relieved her sexual tension.

For three hours, Jo struggled with the wire, managing to fence in another forty feet. Jo's arms ached. She wiped her perspiring forehead with her bandanna. *That's enough for today,* she thought. *I don't want to fall asleep in Brad's arms again.* A smile crossed her lips, as she anticipated the satisfaction he'd promised.

Jo looked down at her hands. They were bleeding and scratched, her nails broken and jagged, her palms callused and rough. *I'm a mess*, she moaned. Her hands darted up to her face. The skin felt soft, but it was covered with a damp veil of perspiration. "I've let myself go," she whispered in shame. Suddenly she was afraid there wasn't enough time to make her body as feminine as the feelings that now raced within it. Jo picked up the tools and made her way toward the barn.

Ruben helped her secure the stallion and Little Girl in the barn. Thunderstorms threatened and the electric fences would have to be turned off. Jo fumed under her breath, *of all times to have to bring the fifteen mares into the barn. It will take over an hour, and tomorrow I'll be left with seventeen stalls to muck out.* Jo steadied her nerves. She'd learned long ago that the only way her work got done was by pushing herself. She and Ruben walked out toward the far pasture to lead the mares safely inside. "Ruben," she said as they walked alongside each other, "how are you feeling? Are you working too hard?"

Ruben glanced over at her. "Nope," he answered in his usual few words.

"Then, what's worrying you? You seem upset."

Ruben turned to her, stopping his wide gait. "You got no pop, no colt, no man. I'm old. Hate to see you so alone, that's all."

Jo was touched by his concern. "I've got you; you're like my pop now."

"I'm gonna die someday, Jo. Then what?"

Jo's mouth dropped open. "Are you all right, Ruben?"

"I'm just old, Jo," he mumbled, concern written on his face. "I'm just worrying about you."

Jo touched his shoulder gently. "I'll be okay, Ruben. I bounce back, remember?"

Ruben resumed walking as he answered, "Time to stop bouncing, Jo. Time to start settling down, like your filly."

Jo smiled at his honest concern and her thoughts turned to Brad. She shook her head, trying to erase them. She'd daydreamed about a future with one man long ago, trusting that he shared her dreams. He'd walked away from her, leaving her as unsatisfied in life as he had in bed. Jo was determined not to get caught up in daydreams over Brad. She knew he was here for a few months and could only offer moments of ecstasy. "Don't worry, Ruben. I don't need anybody, just my horses; remember?"

They continued their walk toward the mares in silence. Ruben had said more to her than he had muttered in a month. Jo knew he'd say no more.

The mares smelled the rain in the air, so they were skittish. It took Jo longer than she'd thought to get them into the barn. When she finally closed the last stall, she let out a deep sigh. Now she had to fill all the water troughs and it was already five o'clock. She had one pot pie in her freezer; that was it. She'd hoped to go to the store and stock up on groceries in case Brad came in time for dinner. She filled her bucket and started toward the first stall. It was going to be a long time before she could even soak in her bath. Preparing a dinner was out of the question.

Jo checked in on Little Girl and the goat. The filly was quietly lying down, the goat's head on her stomach. Jo felt a lump grow in her throat as she studied the two animals that were able to erase the loneliness within each other.

Jo settled down into the bath water and sighed. It felt good to soak her tired muscles. She ran her fingers over her body. It was tight and trim from all the hard work she did. She was unashamed to share it with Brad. She dumped some bubble bath into the water, a long unused Christmas present from an aunt who lived far away. Jo smiled to herself. She wondered what her aunt would think if she knew that horses and manure were her usual perfume.

Jo washed and conditioned her long hair. It felt like silk as she ran it through her fingers. She filed her nails and polished them with pink polish. It was thick from age, but it went on smoothly, so she painted her toenails. Admiring her work, she thought, *what do you know? I clean up pretty well.*

She scanned her wardrobe for something to wear. She owned dress clothes, but they were either outdated or suits. Her eyes caught sight of a white, silk blouse. She pulled it out and slipped it over her head. It was five years old, worn only once to her college graduation. Without a bra, her nipples showed through the silk like two shadows waiting to be exposed. She hesitated thinking, *it's too* revealing, *but who am I kidding?* S*exy is the look I want.* She slipped on her newest jeans, leaving the blouse to flow freely over the waistband. Her heartbeat quickened when she wondered, *when will he come?*

Jo was starving. She went into the kitchen and opened the refrigerator. There wasn't much on the shelves, and what was there didn't appeal to her. *The pot pie will take too long,* she decided. *Brad will be here soon.* Jo opted for a peanut better sandwich. "Quick nourishment," she said, hurrying to make it.

Jo washed down her sandwich with a glass of milk. *Oh, no,* she thought, dabbing her mouth. *Now I smell of peanut butter.* She ran to the bathroom to brush her teeth and wash her hands.

Jo walked out onto her front porch. She sat down on the glider. The sun was setting, and it brought back memories of sitting there with her pop. They'd sit there almost every night, talking about her mother, the horses, and the future of Hobby Hill

Farm. The two would rock back and forth, the glider keeping pace with the subject being discussed. She smiled, remembering how they'd practically rock the glider off the porch while he coached her about each section of an approaching race.

The memories, however, made her feel lonelier. The sun set in a fiery ball, taking all the light with it. Now the earth seemed draped in pitch black. The horses were all in the barn; clouds hid the stars. When the grandfather clock rang out 10:00, everything before her looked as empty as she felt.

Jo stood, shaking her head at how pitiful she'd acted. Bright flares of distant lightning and a low rumble warned of the approaching storm. "He's not coming," she said out loud. "He just made a mockery of me." The feeling of rejection brought bitter memories back to her. "No wonder I swore off men," she hissed through clenched teeth. "They're all bastards."

Jo walked inside slamming the door behind her. She turned off the lights and stomped into her bedroom. She pulled her blouse over her head and tugged off her jeans. Too angry to look for a nightgown, she slipped into bed naked, the sheets feeling cold against her warm skin. She shivered. She'd spent her life sleeping alone in the big, oversized bed. Tonight, however, it seemed larger, colder and lonelier.

Jo puffed up her pillow and laid her head down, thinking, *At least I have my dreams; they're all mine. No one can touch them.* Closing her eyes, she recreated her favorite dream: Little Girl and herself racing toward the finish for the victory.

Through her deep sleep, Jo heard the rumbling around her. The bedroom filled with the flashes of the violent storm outside; the rain came in torrents. "Damn," Jo muttered, as she pulled herself out of bed and ran toward the open windows in her bedroom.

The cold rain blew in on her warm skin, bringing her back to the real world. She slammed them down and ran toward the open windows in the living room. She slammed them down, shouting at herself, "Idiot! You knew it was going to rain."

"Jo," a deep voice called from across the room.

She turned, shocked. The house was dark; only bright flashes of the storm's light broke through in random sequences. She spotted a large form standing in the center of the room. "Who's there?" she demanded, shivers running through her body from both fear and cold rain.

"It's me, Brad," he admitted.

Jo strained her eyes to see him, anger keeping her from running into his arms. "A little late, isn't it, Brad? You sneak into my house in the middle of the night? Who do you think you are? I could have a loaded gun in my hand?" she snapped back.

Brad stood still; his feet planted apart, his weight balanced evenly. His eyes hungrily searched the room for her. A flash of light exposed her, a mere second of revelation. He caught a slight image, a blond-haired nymph standing absolutely naked. He tried to focus in on the form, but darkness returned. His pulse quickened, leaving him speechless. Another flash lit her up for his inspection. Her pink skin was bare; her nipples deep rose and aroused. Her eyes were a flash of anger. "I tried to stay away," he said, breaking the silence.

"Why?" she asked.

"You know why," he answered quietly. "I'm temporary, here only until Doc takes over. I can't get caught up in your dreams and your world, and I don't want to cause you more loss."

Jo could feel her heartbeat quicken. He did want her; he hadn't rejected her. "I'm not a fool, Brad. I know that," Jo said without any trace of anger. A loud clap of thunder punctuated her sentence. The house quieted again. "I'm not naive," she continued. "I breed animals, remember? I know when a man says he wants a woman he's talking about her body. I also know we won't have much time together."

The raw honesty of her words flamed his desire. Yet, he felt hurt—hurt and strangely cheated. He thought of her whispered oath of love to the dying colt and cursed himself under his breath. He was confused. Did he want more than just her body? He was angry over both his indecision and her lack of emotion. "I'm leaving," he said, as another flash of lighting exposed what he was going to turn away from. His eyes ran over her, taking advantage of the moments of light to drink in her visual beauty.

Before he could leave, another flash lit up the room. Before the flash dissolved, Brad looked and saw that Jo was moving in his direction. He stood frozen in expectation, smelling her perfume as she approached. He felt her hands on his face and he thought, *Small hands, but strong like her.* Her fingers traced his features, lightly touching his forehead, then across his eyebrows, down his nose. They gently caressed his cheeks, and then his ears, exposing an erogenous zone he didn't know he possessed. A gasp escaped from his lips until hers pressed against them.

The atmosphere erupted into massive electrostatic discharges, causing loud, sharp clashes of thunder. Brad's body reacted, at first protective and then with pure, erotic need. He pulled her bare body against him, his tongue pushing in between her lips, searching for her moist warmth and intimate taste. She opened to admit him, groaning as her tongue stroked his.

His hands rubbed up her back, smooth skin, strong, lean muscles. His hands moved down, as the passion of their kiss reached new height. He cupped her naked backside pushing it against his loin and she felt his need. Jo groaned again and then their lips parted.

"I want you more than I've ever wanted anything or anyone in my life," he said in a hoarse voice.

"You promised me satisfaction," Jo said as she draped her hands around his neck and lifted her legs to encircle his waist, "I'm yours for the taking." He walked to her bedroom, dizzy with the intoxication of the woman.

Jo was swept away by an untamed biological urge that she had never known. The power of her throbbing, bodily need was accentuated by the violent storm surrounding them. He lowered her into the bed and she arched toward him. He pulled away, opting to kneel on the floor beside the bed. Only his hands remained, rubbing gently down her neck until they found her breasts. They roamed over them, touching, caressing, and lifting each breast. His lips found her erect nipples and he sucked on each one, his tongue flicking against their tip. Then his hands left her, a moment of panic arouse. She listened and smiled when she heard him unzipping his pants, the belt hitting the floor, his shoes being kicked off, and his shirt following the shoes. She sensed the man in her bedroom was now naked, and the flashing lightening confirmed it. She saw Brad, endowed with a magnificent body, fully capable of satisfying all her needs.

Jo lifted her arms toward him and he lowered himself down on top of her. "I should take more time," he said, "but Jo. I want you now."

The storm provided the musical score for their lovemaking. It crescendoed, quieted, and then rose again with new fervor. After several hours, the storm moved away from the farm, leaving Jo and Brad spent and sleeping in each other's arms.

Seven

Jo rose before Brad. She slipped quietly out of the bed, a small smile on her lips. She wrapped her robe around her body and hugged her arms across her chest. Her eyes rested on Brad's face. He was lost in some peaceful dream, a look of contentment making his features seem at rest. Jo memorized his face. He was no longer a stranger to her, he was her lover. Suddenly, the reality of daybreak brought the truth. *He's not your lover,* she scolded herself. *He's temporary.* Jo strode out of the bedroom; there was work to be done.

Brad came into the barn, bellowing like a bull. "You've got no food in that kitchen of yours." His eyes ran over her body, remembering all the delicious curves he'd discovered.

Jo leaned against her pitchfork. "Here I stand with fourteen more stalls to muck out, and the man wants food?" Her eyes glistened as he moved closer. His expression was one of hunger, but not for food. A shiver ran through her.

"Where's Ruben?" he asked carefully.

"He's taking the mares out to pasture," Jo laughed, as Brad slipped his arms around her waist pulling her next to him. "Just what are you hungry for?" she teased. "You seem to have an insatiable appetite."

Brad nibbled on her ear, sending quivers up her spine. His hand reached down and swatted her backside. "Yes, but now I need food—food for strength." He held her at arm's length and ran a finger over her cheek, saying, "A man needs more than love to survive."

Jo's eyes darted up to his face. "Don't say that," she warned, anger filling her. "Don't even kid around about it."

Brad looked into her eyes, spotting panic in the deep, brown pools. His hands gripped her waist as she tried to pull away. "If you don't want to hear it, I won't," he said carefully.

Brad released her, turning away from her anger. "Food, woman!" he bellowed. "I'll muck the stalls, if you get some groceries and make breakfast."

Jo watched him carefully, her heart racing. She flipped her hair over her shoulders thinking, *how dare he pretend to care. I wonder if he tells everyone he sleeps with that he loves her. Probably thinks it's required.* "I'll get you the food," she said, starting toward the barn door. "By the way," she asked while turning back, "just what do I feed you two goats?"

Brad stared up at her, a smile running across his face. "So you've decided we have value, after all."

Jo's eyes danced with her answer. "Why, yes. You seem to keep the females busy enough to stop their stall-walking."

Brad threw his head back and laughed. "Okay, then. Bacon and eggs for me, and the other animal will eat goat feed and anything else it gets close to."

Jo threw her hands up in mock disgust, saying, "That's just great. Now I have to feed my goat special grain, my horse barbecue chips, and my..." her voice trailed off.

Brad urged her on. "Your what, Jo?"

"Why, my stud. Did you say bacon and eggs?"

An hour later, Jo returned to the barn. She carried a fifty-pound sack of goat feed with her, straining her back against the load. Brad spotted her and dropped his pitchfork. "Don't, Jo," he said as he moved toward her. "You'll hurt yourself."

Jo's eyes shot up and she warned him, "I carry my own weight around here. Always have. I'm stronger than you think. I'm short but mighty. Back away, buddy."

Brad turned back to the last stall, avoiding watching her. Jo opened the bag and filled a bucket with goat feed. She walked up to Brad, suggesting, "Let's see if your goat takes to this."

"That goat will take anything you wish to dish out," Brad said. "It's not as stubborn as you."

"You think I'm stubborn?" Jo asked as they walked up to the stall.

"You? You're the most dogged determined person I ever met. Pigheaded, but on you, it looks good," Brad said as he laid his hand on her shoulder.

"I live in a man's world. If I'd listened to all the men who gave me bad advice, I'd never be running this ranch," Jo explained.

Brad turned and waved his arm toward the goat announcing, "And then there's me. I only give good advice."

"About that goat," Jo said more seriously. "Should I let him go out in the field with Little Girl?"

"Of course. They're buddies now; you can't split them up. Just give your goat a few minutes with this feed and we'll let them out," Brad said smiling as he watched the goat attack the bucket of food.

"What do you call this thing, anyway?" Jo asked.

"It's your goat. Call it anything you want," Brad said, as he ran his hands over Little Girl's legs.

Jo leaned over and stared at the goat. "It's got blue eyes. I think I'll call it Brad," she teased.

"Anything but that," Brad said as he crossed over to Jo. "I thought I proved I wasn't an old goat last night. Besides," he drawled slowly, "it's a nanny goat, or hasn't the fine, horse breeder thought to check that out?"

Jo laughed at the oversight. "Okay, I'll call her Nanny, since her job is to watch over Little Girl and keep her company."

"Very original," Brad teased. His face grew serious and he asked, "What am I to you, Jo? Do you think of me as only a stud?"

Jo walked over to him; she tipped her face up and placed a gentle kiss on his full lips. "You're Brad," she said, the kiss stirring the desire for more, "and you're welcome here whenever you want, preferably not at midnight. You scared me. She leaned away from him, her pulse beginning to climb. "Come, I'll feed you." She headed toward the farmhouse. "Hurry," she warned, "I think Rowdy smells the coffee."

Brad dropped his pitchfork and ran after her, scooping her up in his arms and hoisting her over his shoulder like a sack of feed. "You're an impossible woman," he shouted above her squeals. Her hair flew around his face in waves; it carried their mixed scent.

Brad spent the entire morning at Jo's farm. They enjoyed a leisurely breakfast and then moved back out to work. Brad checked the mares in the field. Jo let Ruben hold the horses while Brad examined them. She needed to put some distance between them.

Jo tried to keep her eyes off the form of the man in the field. She forced herself to go into the barn and hitch up Little Girl for their training session. She couldn't let Brad become so important to her. She had to focus only on her future, Little Girl.

Jo's eyes ran over her filly. She was rested and calm. A chill ran through her. *Perhaps*, she thought, *there is a real chance Little Girl will make it as a racehorse.* Her thought confused her; she'd been unaware of her subconscious doubts. She shook her head absently and led Little Girl toward the track.

As Jo settled into the seat behind the filly, a thrill ran through her. Now she would get to show Brad what Little Girl was really made of. She urged the filly out onto the track, noting that Brad was coming toward them. A smile of satisfaction crossed her lips. It was important to her that Brad sees how wonderful Little Girl was, so he would approve of her breeding. Especially now, since Jo knew Brad had discovered that her four mares were in foal by the same stallion that had sired Little Girl, the unproven stud.

Jo started toward the first turn. Little Girl was ready today. She had a new energy to draw upon, a full night's sleep. The filly threw her head up and burst into a quick trot, her nose drinking in the fresh air as her legs picked up more speed. Jo had meant to show Brad how strong she was, but she was not prepared for this new burst of strength. The filly went the first mile in quick time. Jo had trouble keeping her in a jog. She was afraid she would turn into a real pace. As the filly started the second mile, Jo's eyes spotted Brad for a fleeting moment. He sat on the fence studying the filly as she passed. *He's impressed,* Jo thought, a thrill running through her.

Jo let Little Girl have more speed. She was eager to really show her off. Little Girl's legs began to quicken; the filly was enjoying the session. The second mile was jogged in a faster pace. Jo's hands gripped the reins. She wondered if she should hold the horse back, but pride made her urge the filly on. Brad was watching. Little Girl's hoofs beat out their steady pattern, her legs lifting higher and higher, her nostrils flaring out in excitement. Neither of them had gone so fast together; they both sensed the new accomplishment. At the completion of the second mile, Jo pulled her into a slower trot and urged the filly toward the side.

Jo could feel the flush of her cheeks and she knew her eyes were lit up with excitement. She didn't care. She wanted Brad's approval and she didn't care if he sensed her need. Brad slid off the fence and crossed over to Little Girl. He ran his hands over the animal, taking note of the filly's muscles, her breathing. His first words shook Jo. "Why didn't you push her harder?" he asked seriously. "She had more to give. You're not working her hard enough."

He studied the filly's eyes, looking for enlarged pupils from lack of oxygen. "You should take her at least another two and a half miles. And, Jo, why didn't you turn her and let her go the full pace?"

His questions came like incriminations. Jo was devastated. She had wanted him to see the worth of Little Girl and her breeding, but that was all he saw. Suddenly it was Jo herself who felt like a loser. She hopped out of the seat and jerked her horse away from Brad. "I'm the trainer," she hissed through clenched teeth. "I don't need your insults or questions."

Jo led Little Girl away from Brad. She unhitched the training cart and pulled a blanket over the filly. With a sharp tug, Jo began walking the horse around the paddock, as if to cool it down. Most of all, Jo needed to cool herself down. Nanny followed both of them, eating grass whenever they slowed down.

Brad crossed the track and approached them all. "No need to walk that horse, Jo. The filly's not spent out. Why, she hasn't even gotten her sweat up." Jo turned her head and gave him a warning glare. "What's wrong, Jo?" he said slowly. "I thought you wanted to win. You look like you're training for the loss."

His words came at her like a shock wave. She sent a hateful glare toward the man on the fence. "Get out of here," she hissed through clenched teeth. "Get off my farm."

Brad would not be put off. He climbed off the fence and walked to her side. "I don't leave that easily, Jo," he warned as he approached her. "I don't go away like some fleeting dream." He pulled her against him, ripping the reins out of her hands. He jerked the blanket off the filly's back. "Take a look. The horse is barely in a deep sweat."

Jo turned her eyes from him in anger. She looked over at her filly. He was right. Little Girl looked eager to go on. Her eyes came back to his. He was insulting her. She drew her teeth together and spat out her order. "Get off my farm."

Brad's face changed expression. His mouth turned into a teasing grin. "No, you're not stubborn at all. I'm not some teenager you can order off your property. I'm not some old man who's afraid to hurt your feelings, so he won't tell you the truth. I'm Brad, remember? The man you said was welcome here anytime, the man who made love to you last night." He pulled her into his arms, dragging her fighting body next to his.

She pounded her fists on his back, dug her nails into his shoulders. "Let me go. I hate you."

Brad ran his hand over her hair and whispered into her ear. "Face it, Jo. You're just scared to find out just how quick Little Girl really is. You're scared she'll hurt herself like your other two dream horses. Jo, you can't win the race if you don't believe."

Brad's words came to her like bullets, killing the enemy of doubt. He was right, and he cared enough to take her insults and show her. She stopped fighting against his grasp and leaned into his broad shoulders and strong arms. She needed his strength, his confidence, and his honesty.

His lips ran lightly over her cheek. "Did I tell you what a hell of a good driver you are? Did I tell you how you make me want to throw you down on the ground and take you right here?" His words increased her need. She offered her lips to him. He brought his mouth down hard upon hers, proving his admiration and desire. His hands rubbed her back gently, then, realizing Ruben might see them, he pulled himself away.

"Thanks, Brad," she whispered through moist lips. "Thanks for caring."

"You've got a winner there, Jo," he answered, winking one eye. "You just have to want to see it." Brad released her and turned to leave.

"Aren't you going to tell me what to do?" she asked, suddenly anxious for his suggestions.

"You know already, Jo," he answered as he climbed the fence and walked away. "You've just got to decide that you're ready."

Jo watched as he walked through the field toward the mares. His words ran through her mind. With shaking hands, she hitched Little Girl up again. She opened the track gate and led the horse in. Her heart was pounding with fear as she gripped the reins. She let Little Girl jog one more time around the track, bringing her body heat up to the level of excitement. Brad stopped his walking and returned to the track. Ruben followed, his aged steps coming slower.

Jo took a deep breath and gave the signal for Little Girl to turn the right way for the race. The filly's legs began to fly as she broke into a fast pace. The dirt under the wheels turned into powder as Jo sped by. Little Girl pushed on, her hoofs pounding harder, her legs increasing speed. Jo's hands shook, but still she urged Little Girl on. She was fast—faster than the colt, Jupiter, faster than even the stallion. Little Girl had heart, not just speed. She had heart! Jo let the horse pace her own speed, her eyes flashing in excitement as she bounced behind in the training bike. Her mind raced along, thinking my *dreams could come true. Little Girl could do it!*

Brad and Ruben yelled Whoopee and Way to Go! They pounded one another on the back and waved their hats in the air as she passed them. Jo and her filly had made the turn. They were finally headed in the right direction, racing toward their future with determination.

Eight

It had been a good day—a wonderful day—and Jo was elated. She shoved lasagna into the oven, suddenly wondering if southerners like Italian food. It had been so long since she'd prepared a meal for company that she'd forgotten how much she enjoyed cooking. She usually just grabbed something for herself after a long, hard day of work. With Brad's help, all the work was done and she had free time. Jo carried a pitcher of iced tea out to the patio, eager to get close to the man who had made the day so perfect.

Brad sat on the brick wall surrounding the patio, his gaze fixed. He smiled as she came into view. "How many acres do you have, Jo?" he asked, accepting the tea.

Jo settled down in a chair, pulling her boots off and wiggling her toes. "Two hundred and fifty," she answered proudly. "It used to be a diary farm, that's why I have such a huge barn. Then, when Dad realized there were no more kids coming along to help him with all the work, he started switching over to horses. I think he knew I could handle the work around a small horse farm, but cows are another thing.

Jo sipped her tea and felt it chill her throat. "Do you know that cows have to be milked twice a day and just the thought of mucking out a cow barn brings tears to my eyes? Cow dung really stinks. If you get a hot spell, the cows have to live in the barn; and we had to spray them down with hoses. They can't take the heat. What a mess; then there's the breeding. If you want milk, cows have to be bred. If you want to make any money selling your milk, you better have a big herd of cows. And dumb," she laughed, "cows are dumb."

Brad laughed along with her. "They're dumb, but they're gentle," he said kindly. "Horses can be dangerous, especially driving them like you do. No wonder your dad insisted you get good training."

Jo was grateful to hear him approve of her background. It pleased her after his earlier comments at the track. "I feel wonderful tonight," Jo said, reaching her arms over her head, stretching out her back. "You can ask me anything you want; I'm a wealth of information tonight."

Brad smiled warmly. "All right; just what breed is that mangy dog of yours? I never saw an uglier creature."

Jo laughed as she glanced across the field toward Rowdy. "He's half English bulldog, one-quarter bull mastiff and one-quarter pit bull. I got him from a friend of mine in college. She thought it would be a great senior project to breed bulldogs backwards, toward the pure bull breed. He was a generation on the way. He's a character, but he's all mine and I love him." She watched as Rowdy dove into the pond, missing a frog miserably. She laughed.

Brad smiled with her. "You know, Jo, your four mares are well in foal. If Little Girl proves herself on the track, you're going to be on your way toward a good strong horse farm. I'm happy for you."

Jo smiled. It felt good having someone believe in her dreams, someone she could talk to, and someone she could make love to. Everything about Brad was good. *Maybe too good*, she worried. "Brad," she asked, trying to be causal, "how long will you be here?"

Brad lifted his glass and took a sip, before saying, "I'm not sure. Doc may decide to retire now that he's had this heart attack. That'll mean his practice will be up for grabs. I've some money saved but not enough to buy it. I guess I'll just stay until he decides what he wants to do."

Jo felt the stab of reality deflate the joy of the day. *He's going to leave*, she thought. Jo put her glass down, afraid to look over at him. "Where will you go?" she asked, trying to sound light. "Does your family have a ranch? You said your uncle had one, didn't you?"

Brad shook his head slowly, his gaze still on the mares. "Yes, Jo, but he has a pack of sons going into the business. No, I don't have a home to go back to. I'll have to fill in for another vet until I save up enough money to strike out on my own or get hired by a big horse farm down south. I have more contacts down there."

Jo thought awhile. She knew the farms around town hired full-time vets. Hanover, Pennsylvania, was well-known for famous pacers and trotters as the lime in the soil made their bones stronger. All the large farms already had vets, vets set for life. Old Doc's practice served the smaller farms such as hers, and Doc had developed a good rapport with his clients. Brad was right— they would refer only to the vet who bought Doc's practice. They would respect his right to sell his practice and trust in his professional selection.

"How much do you think Doc will ask for his practice?" Jo said sadly.

About twenty thousand more than I have," Brad answered. He rose, placing his glass down beside him. "No more talk of money. Today is a happy day, remember? Let's join Rowdy for a swim."

Jo was now depressed. Brad would leave; he had to. "Not now," she said slowly. "I don't feel up to it."

Brad pulled her up into his arms. "What, not up to it? I thought you were up to any challenge."

"Brad!" Jo squealed, as he threw her over his shoulder and headed for the pond. "I have my clothes on."

"Move over, Rowdy," Brad called out, increasing his speed. "I've got one little frog to throw back in."

They hit the water together, Jo screaming in astonishment. They sank to the bottom, Brad keeping his arms around her waist. He lifted her to the surface, making sure she got air. Jo gasped, her lungs aching from laughter and loss of oxygen.

"You're insane," she yelled, pushing him back under the water.

Brad came back up to the surface, his face drenched with water and amusement. "Don't complain," he warned. "At least you have your boots off." He moved next to her, taking her in his arms. "Now, about the rest of you," he said suggestively. His fingers began unbuttoning her shirt. "Don't you think you should get out of these wet clothes?" A grin crossed his lips.

Jo narrowed her eye dramatically. "Why, when I'm still in the water?"

"Well," he continued, "then maybe I'll get out of mine. I've heard that skinny dipping can be quite a lot of fun." He finished unbuttoning the blouse and slowly moved the wet material apart. Her naked breasts floated up and he stared at them, saying, "Beautiful. Do you mind if I touch them?"

Joe slipped her blouse off her shoulder and threw it up on shore. She turned back to him and stared into his blue eyes, urging, "Please Brad, touch me, touch me now."

His hands gently caressed and kneaded her naked breasts. The warmth of his hands in contrast with the cool water ignited her passion. The sensation was beyond expectation. He gently lifted and moved her toward him so his lips could take her nipple into his warm mouth. Jo threw back her head and groaned. Never in all her life could she have imagined such sensations, such pleasure, and such lust. "Brad, please. I want to feel your body, naked and next to me. Take your clothes off."

They lifted themselves onto the shore and jerked their wet clothes off. Then holding hands, they jumped back into the pond.

The film of water lubricated their bodies so the sensation of being naked was new and intoxicating. They slid against each other, in a clumsy ballet of exploration. She teased him by swimming behind him, pushing her breasts and lower body against him, her hands reaching around his waist to feel his sexual reaction.

Under the water, nothing seemed off limits. Only their faces remained on the surface now inches apart, staring and watching each other's reaction as their hands fondled, caressed, stroked and probed. The pure, natural responses seen on their lovers' faces removed inhibitions. Intimacy was raw, honest and intense, until finally, they became one, wrapped in each other's arms while leaning on the grassy shoreline. They lay, half their bodies still in the water, unwilling to break the union.

When they parted, they pulled out of the pond and lay on the grass, both emotionally and physically spent. The sun dried their bodies as they both breathed in deeply, only their hands joined. Their perfect minutes of rest and rejuvenation, however, ended abruptly as Brad jerked up at the sound. Rowdy had found his wet boots and was busily attacking them as if they were live animals.

Brad was on his feet, grabbing for one boot now in Rowdy's mouth. Rowdy thought he'd invented a new game and began to run around Brad in big, irregular circles.

Jo sat up and laughed. "You're both nuts," she called out. She stood, picked up the one boot and all the other clothes. "When you two are done playing around," she said still laughing, "I'll have dinner ready."

"Aren't you going to help me?" Brad asked. "This beast is not giving in."

"All right," Jo said dramatically. "He's really easy to deal with. Watch this," Jo said, putting down the pile of clothes. "Come on Rowdy, let's swim."

Brad watched in amazement as Rowdy dropped his boot and followed Jo back into the pond. "Now I get it," Brad called out. "He was jealous and look who won. He's got you in the water and I'm left with a wet boot."

"Poor Rowdy," Jo said as she emerged from the pond. "We ruined his day. All the frogs have gone in hiding."

Brad watched as she approached him, her wet skin glistening in the sunlight. "Do you know that you take my breath away? You're so beautiful," Brad explained.

"And stubborn; I am stubborn," Jo said, as she took his hand and they walked to the farmhouse.

"You are that. You're a handful even though you are small," Brad said.

"I'll take that as an offhand compliment," Jo admitted.

"Food!" Brad yelled, as they approached the house. "I smell delicious food. I need food after a shower."

"I'm first, Jo said. "I'm the cook."

"Why don't we take a shower together?" Brad suggested, his hand lowering to caress Jo's bare backside.

"I thought you were hungry?" Jo said.

"But there's something about holding you in water that makes me forget even food," Brad decided, as he held the front door open for Jo.

Jo lit the candle on the patio picnic table. Brad watched her carry out the food and then the wine. "Your job tonight," she said smiling. "Uncork the wine and cut the garlic bread."

"Is that all you want from me?" Brad asked.

"The night is young," she said, holding two glasses. "There might be more."

"I certainly hope so," Brad said, as he poured the red wine into their glasses. "I think I should clear the table and do the dishes."

"I'll take you up on that," Jo announced, clicking her glass against his. "Here's to the best day of my life," Jo toasted. Brad was stunned by her words. He stared at her noticing the tears in her eyes. *I am falling in love with this woman, and I can't seem to stop myself,* he thought as he turned away to hide the rush of emotions within him.

While they devoured the lasagna, they talked about each of her mares, the goat and Rowdy. As Brad stood to remove the dishes, he asked, "What will you do while I wash dishes?" He didn't want the flow of their conversation to break off.

Entertain you," Jo said smiling.

"You always entertain me," Brad admitted. "What do you have in mind?"

"You'll see," she said, as she helped carry things inside to the kitchen. After putting them on the sink, she walked over and lifted the old leather case leaning in the corner. She opened it while he stood watching. "I'm about to astonish you with my ability on the guitar. Don't expect me to sing; I'm strictly a musician. You can listen while I tune up and play on the porch."

He stared as she lifted the guitar from the case and draped the strap over her shoulder. He stood, spellbound, as she smiled and walked to the patio, her long, blonde hair swinging. *I can hardly breathe*, Brad noticed.

Brad watched as Jo perched herself on the patio wall, cradling her guitar with one leg. He smiled as she tuned up the guitar and then turned to begin his task. By the time the dishes were cleaned, she was strumming familiar tunes and gentle cords. He refilled their wine glasses and sat in the chair watching her. The evening breeze blew her hair. It lifted like a running horse's mane. Everything about her seemed magical. The stars lit up the field, showing the mares roaming freely. The night air filled with the blended sound of her guitar music and the neighs of her horses. Brad's heart pounded heavily. She was everything he had ever wanted in life. He too was having the best day of his life, but he couldn't tell her. She belonged to this farm, and he would someday have to leave them behind.

Brad's heart soared as she played a song whose title now eluded him. All he could remember was the chorus, and it was all about coming home. When she finished, he reached over and gently touched her cheek.

Jo lifted her guitar strap off her shoulder, and smiled warmly. "Let's go to bed, Brad," she whispered. He followed her, trying to memorize the sway of her perfect backside.

Nine

Brad rolled over and kissed Jo lightly on her forehead. "I've got to go," he announced, before standing up. "You're ruining my career."

Jo stretched lazily, opening her eyes to discover the early morning light. "Spoilsport," she said, her words still hoarse from sound sleep. She watched him as he pulled his shirt over his broad shoulders. "Be glad I have a dryer," she teased. "I could have sent you out into the cold, morning air in damp clothes. By the way, where do you go when you're not breaking into my house?" Her eyes sparkled with fresh interest.

Brad reached over to gently move a strand of her hair off her forehead. "I live in a cave with a family of wolves up in the Pigeon Hills," he taunted back.

Jo threw a pillow at him. "Now don't kid me. You may be a wolf, but not the cave-dwelling kind." She lowered her hands over her face, bracing against the returning pillow. "Where do you live? Do you live with Doc's wife while he's in the hospital?"

Brad threw his head back and laughed. "Doc was glad for me to cover his practice, but he never invited me to move in with his wife. Besides, she's too old for me, probably near seventy." He finished buttoning his shirt. "I rent an apartment over the old furniture store on Baltimore Street. You know, the one that's now a twirling studio." He kissed her lightly on her lips preparing to leave.

Jo sat up in bed, her face displaying her amazement. "Oh Brad," she laughed, "They practice every night. How can you stand all those marches and pop records blaring through your floor?" She pushed her hair back, trying to imagine Brad living there; "There's no grass there, only concrete. You must hate it there."

Brad brought his lips against her cheek, kissing her gently. "That's why the rent is dirt cheap. I'm not there very often, remember?" he said suggestively. "It's just a place to change my clothes and store my food. Believe it or not," he ran a finger down her neck, "I have a lot of horses that keep me very busy, and now there's you."

His eyes conveyed the depth of feeling he was developing for her; she missed it, too busy enjoying the feel of his finger tracing down her neck and over her breasts.

"So it's me or the twirlers," she whispered slowly. "Can I expect you tonight, or will you opt for marches and thumps?"

Brad answered mysteriously, "It's neither place tonight." His eyes watched as her face revealed disappointment. "Tonight I'm off to a party at Hanover's biggest horse farm." He turned his back to her, hoping she would ask questions. She was quiet, accepting defeat too easily. "Everyone will be there—all the owners, vets, and trainers. You know one of those big parties no one in the business misses. Most of the drivers you'll be racing against at the fair will show up." He turned to study her face.

"Oh," she said softly. "I wasn't invited, you know. Ever since my stallion was hurt, they don't consider me in the business." Jo sat cross-legged in the center of the bed, her long hair draped over her thin, naked body, her large eyes staring down at the bed-spread pulled over her legs. *She gives up too easily,* Brad thought. He walked over to the bed, sitting down next to her. "Well, what would you say if we shocked them with the truth? You know, announced to everyone that not only are you in the business, but come September you'll be driving the sulky behind the fastest horse on the track?"

Jo's eyes rose to meet his. "Do you mean you'd take me to the party? Wouldn't that hurt your rapport with the other owners?"

Brad laughed at her concern for him. "I never met a horseman who didn't appreciate a beautiful woman, and you take the prize in that category," he said, kissing her lips.

Jo's heartbeat quickened. Brad thought she was beautiful, and he was going to escort her back into the fold of harness racing. "I'd have to get a dress," she said, her mind racing with excitement. "A real knockout," she continued. "Some of those riders boxed me in during the race that hurt my stallion. There's one, Sam Randolph, a driver for Fairview Hill Farm, who drove me into the fence." Her eyes darkened as she remembered the day. "Did you know I protested the race? I would have won, everyone said so, but they didn't take films of the southwest curve. It was my word against his—the liar and cheat. He cost me my stallion's health and something much worse. Just wait till I see him again. I'll show him he's in for trouble."

Brad listened quietly, a slight grin coming to his face. "You seem to be getting your dander up. Will you behave yourself if I take you to the party?"

Jo tossed her hair back over her shoulders. "Don't worry, Brad. I'll be the perfect lady. Last time I drove with all of them, I was just a green kid. I was heartbroken when my horse was injured, sobbed for hours. Both my dad and I were devastated. Then, two weeks later, dad died of a heart attack."

"Jo, I had no idea," Brad said stunned.

"Every one of those drivers came to his funeral. Most apologized for treating Dad and me so badly at the track—everyone but Sam Randolph. He wouldn't show his face." Jo punched her fist into the bed. "Everyone told me to get out of the business. It was much too hard for a young girl like me to handle alone." Jo lifted her chin up and she glared at Brad. "I'll go, but this time they'll see a woman who's grown up and ready to challenge them. This time they won't see my tears, just my dust."

Brad was still in shock with all she had handled on her own but knew better than to mention it. "Remind me," he said softly, "never to cross you. I think you could be as dangerous as you are stubborn." He rose from the bed and started toward the door. "I'll pick you up around 8:00. It's formal, you know, tux and long gowns and all that stuff." He tilted his head, closing one eye.

"What in the world are you doing?" Jo called out, throwing the pillow one more time.

He caught it and threw it back, hitting her across the face. "Oh, nothing. I was just trying to picture what in the world you'd look like in a dress." He shrugged and walked out the door.

Jo listened as his footsteps faded. Her heart pounded with her plans. "He'll see me in a dress," she thought mischievously "The most beautiful gown I can get my hands on. I'll shock them all. I'll show them that Jo Martin is now a woman, a woman come of age, and a real winner."

By ten o'clock, she had jogged Little Girl for four miles. It was standard training practice to give a horse two days at a slow jog, and then one at full speed. Today was one of the lighter training days, and Jo was glad she would have some free time. She walked over to Ruben as he swept out the barn. "Ruben," she began, "I've got to go into town. Brad is taking me to a big shindig at one of the horse farms. I've got some shopping to do."

Ruben looked up from his work, a small grin on his face. "Good," he said awkwardly. "Have fun." He turned back to his work, his face seeming happier. *He's happy because I'm going out,* she thought. *I bet he's seen enough to know that Brad and I are in a relationship.* Part of her wanted to warn Ruben not to get his hopes up, to tell him that Brad would leave someday. Jo couldn't bring herself to say the words so she turned and walked slowly out of the barn.

Jo entered the boutique feeling uneasy. It smelled of expensive perfume, sparkled with jewelry, shoes and racks of feminine dresses. These were unfamiliar things to Jo; these were the luxuries her lifestyle avoided. Mrs. Van Order came out of the back, stirred from her bookwork by the sound from the small bell on the door. The older woman had been her mother's close friend so now Jo felt safe and more comfortable. Mrs. Van Order's face displayed her pleasure at seeing Jo. Her arms reached out to hug her tenderly. "Jo," she said gently, "I'm so pleased you've come to see me. It's been so long since we've had a chance to chat."

Jo smiled to herself. It never dawned on the elegant woman that Jo had come to buy one of her gowns. "Hello, Mrs. Van Order," Jo began. "I've come for your expert advice. I need a gown that makes me look mature and sophisticated." Her eyes watched, as the face of the older woman grew intense with interest. "I've been invited to an important party at one of the big horse farms, and I need to make an entrance they won't forget."

Mrs. Van Order clasped her hands together enthusiastically. "Oh, my," she sighed in delight. "I've been waiting for this day! If you had gone to anyone but me, I'd have rung your neck. This is one commission I'll forfeit. I'm going to help you make an entrance that will knock this town off its feet." She squeezed Jo's hands, reassuring her. "I've got a dress that will be beautiful on you. I'll sell it at cost; just don't tell anyone about it." She walked around Jo, eyeing her body. "You're probably a size two, just perfect for it." Her hands reached up and stroked Jo's long hair. "You're so beautiful; it's as if this gown was created just for you."

Jo smiled as the woman disappeared into the back room. She was grateful to have the help of a friend she trusted. The life Jo led did not give her much time for shopping trips. She was out of touch with the news of the fashion world, couldn't even remember the last time she'd worn nylons.

Mrs. Van Order emerged with a long turquoise gown, covered with plastic. The woman had taken charge. "This is a mermaid style evening gown, made of silk. It's perfect to show off your beautiful body. What size shoes do you wear?" she asked, as she pulled off the protective cover.

"A five, Jo answered, her eyes mesmerized by the yards of flowing fabric in the woman's hands. It cascaded like a Caribbean waterfall from the velvet hanger.

Mrs. Van Order showed Jo into a dressing room and hung the gown on a hook. Jo reached out to touch the magnificent gown. Mrs. Van Order closed the curtain and left. She returned a few minutes later with a strapless, padded foundation garment saying, "Wear this. It will cinch in your waist and push up your breasts. Let's throw caution out the window. Now get started while I find you shoes."

A thrill ran through Jo, and she pulled off her shirt, boots and jeans. She sucked in her breath and squeezed into the corset, fastening the hooks. Her breasts suddenly looked plump and voluptuous. Jo took a deep breath and slipped the gown off the hanger. She closed her eyes and lifted the cool fabric over her head. It felt soft, like gossamer, next to her skin. It slid down her back, resting on her breasts. She reached behind easily zipping up the back.

Jo opened her eyes and gasped. The gown had no straps, no sleeves, and no frills. It was a simple design, a strapless sheath that clung to her half-exposed breasts and fitted her 18-inch waist, making her curves all the decoration needed. The bottom of the gown slid over her hips and buttocks. It fit perfectly without appearing tight and ending in swirls of fabric that rustled with her movements. When she turned to see the back, she gasped. The view from the back was as sexy and revealing as the one from the front. It exposed her toned back and the shape of her butt.

Jo turned around and studied herself. The turquoise color made her eyes jet black, her hair golden, and her suntanned skin glowing. Jo breathed out a sigh. She knew this was the perfect gown. Mrs. Van Order pulled the curtain aside, offering her a pair of silver heels. Jo slipped them on, uneasy at wearing such delicate shoes. She walked out of the dressing room, lifting the hem ever so lightly.

As the light of the day exposed her, Jo notice the look of astonishment on Mrs. Van Order's face. Tears came to the woman's eyes. "If only Ruth could see you," she whispered, thinking of her lost friend, Jo's mother. She cleared her throat and extended her hands. "Come look in the three-way mirror. You're absolutely beautiful."

Jo walked to view her reflection. She stared at herself in surprise. She did look beautiful! A new confidence flowed through her, and she forgot about the men she would meet at the party and the race she wanted to win. Jo thought only of Brad and the possibility that perhaps he could fall in love with her. Her heart skipped a beat. If he only loved her, maybe they could find a way for him to stay in Hanover. Maybe they could have a life together.

Jo turned and threw her arms around the older woman beside her. "I love it," she admitted. "It's just perfect."

Mrs. Van Order carefully pinned up the hem. She instructed her seamstress to drop all other work and adjust the gown. Then she laced her arm through Jo's and swept her out the door toward the drug store. "We've got to get some makeup," she ordered in her motherly tone. "Just a little color to accent those beautiful eyes of yours."

Jo smiled and put her faith in the hand of this wizard of fashion. Jo Martin was suddenly game for anything if it meant winning Brad's love.

When Jo returned home, she carried an armload of boxes in her hands. They were bulky, but lighter than the sacks of feed she was used to dragging around. Jo laid them carefully on the bed, her heart pounding. She lifted the soft, turquoise gown from its box and hung it in her closet. She laid out the silver shoes, her fingers running over the delicate straps. She pulled the small, silver bag from its wrapping, carefully taking out the tissue paper and then her lace corset. Finally, Joe opened a tiny box holding two small pearl earrings, the first jewelry she had ever bought.

Jo laid her makeup on the bathroom counter, soft hues of gray and deep brown to dress up her eyes, blush to heighten the color of her cheeks and pale, pink lipstick. Jo studied them carefully. She had worn makeup years ago, when she'd been in college and eager to attract the attention of men. She hadn't worn it since, putting it aside when her first encounter with a man had proved a failure. Jo touched the row of trappings with anticipation. She was willing to try again, to take another chance at love, to dream of a future with Brad.

Jo turned away. She had work to do. It was only three o'clock, and she had to jog Little Girl again. The filly's stamina needed to be built up. Jo walked slowly out of the bedroom, leaving all the beautiful clothes behind.

As Jo led the horse toward the track, she noticed that the goat followed. She smiled. A bond had been forged between the two animals, and they were happiest when together. Jo thought of Brad. She hoped a bond of more than sex was beginning to weave them together. Jo missed him, even though they had been apart for only a few hours. A lump came to her throat. Suddenly, Jo realized that she truly loved the man, an emotion she had tried to avoid. Her hand shook as she led the horse closer to the track. She had two challenges to face—the race with Little Girl, and the race for Brad. Fear ran through her at the thought of losing either one.

As Jo hitched her filly up to the training cart, she remembered Brad's words. "You train to lose. You have to believe you can win." Jo flipped her hair up under the helmet, a new Jo emerging. She decided to train to win, to go for both the winner's cup and Brad. Jo settled onto the seat in her bike. She slapped the reins on the filly's back and started to train for victory.

Ten

Brad stood in the center of Jo's living room, his eyes glued to the woman in front of him. She was sexy, yet elegant. Her golden hair was wrapped into a soft swirl on top of her head, two earrings accentuating her tiny ear lobes. Her eyes seemed darker, more alluring and worldly. Brad sighed as his eyes ran down her body. Memories of her emerging naked from the pond, her body glistening in the sun, made this image even more enticing. Now she looked like a mermaid, just risen from the Caribbean waters. He shuddered, realizing she'd fill every man with yearning. Jo now possessed the mystique of a mature woman who knew exactly what and how she was doing.

Brad smiled faintly, thinking of the first day they had met. How could he have missed that she was a woman? How could he have thought her a mere child? An image ran through his mind, a picture of her dressed in her everyday jeans with her long hair braided. He ran his hand over his lips, readjusting to the new image standing before him.

Jo couldn't wait any longer. She walked slowly toward him, the long gown rustling on the floor as she moved. "You haven't said a word," she pointed out. "Don't I even get a soft, wolf whistle?" She brought her pink lips close to his, closing her eyes in expectation.

Brad reached over and drew her into his arms. His kiss was filled with burning passion, melting away her doubt. His body demonstrated his urgent desire. Brad pulled away, looking dazed and confused. His hands rose to gently run over her breasts, the filmy fabric allowing their warmth to penetrate through to his fingertips. She shivered and moved closer, wanting more, much more.

Brad reacted by placing his hands on her bare shoulders, holding her a few inches from his body. "Don't push me, Jo," he warned, in a thick, unfamiliar tone. "Right now, I don't want to share you with anyone, especially a room filled with other men. If you have any intention of going to that damn party, don't be so willing." His eyes looked into hers, and she saw the struggle he was waging against his own needs.

Jo stepped back a few paces, admitting, "I just wanted to know if you thought I looked all right." A smile formed on her lips as she shrugged and added, "I guess I have my answer." Brad turned away, flipping off a light. "Let's go," he demanded. "Let's get out of here." He strode out the door, leaving Jo speechless and confused. She followed, pulling the door closed.

Brad walked toward the jeep in silence. Rowdy was busy reacquainting himself with the tires. The dog stopped sniffing and sauntered over to Brad, waiting for him to reach down and pat him. Instead, Brad shouted angrily, "Keep away, you ugly mutt. Not now."

Jo's heart sank—something was wrong, terribly wrong. She climbed into the seat, accepting Brad's help. She squeezed his hand, a slight motion meant to bring back their casual relationship. Brad's eyes squinted in warning.

They drove in frozen silence for an intolerable half-hour. Jo stared out the front window, her mind racing; *so he's a jealous man and one with a bad temper. I don't like this side of him.* Jo dabbed on new lipstick. She turned to stare at Brad as he drove. He was dressed in a black tuxedo, his sandy hair looking deeper in color. His face seemed more mature, set in deep, rigid lines. His mouth held no promise of a smile, just a faint line of irritation circling his lips. Jo sighed, turning away.

She took a deep breath, thinking, *I may be stubborn, but he's acting like an insecure fool.* When Jo turned to look again, he glanced at her and smiled ever so lightly. *Maybe he's upset because he knows I have to face the men who hurt me. Maybe he's feeling protective of me.* Jo smiled back, and then turned to focus on the first goal of this evening. *I need to be confident, strong, and coolheaded,* she reminded herself. *My second goal, Brad, will be my reward. In a few hours, we'll be alone and safely in each other's arms.*

The largest horse farm in Hanover was a sight to behold, acre after acre of fences, holding back hundreds of valuable horses. These horses were the pinnacles of good breeding and strong lineage. Some of the horses were valued at millions of dollars.

Jo stared blankly as they drove past the manicured paddocks and professional barns. She steadied her nerves as they turned up the private drive toward the owner's mansion, thinking, *they'll soon see that I've come back grownup and stronger than ever.*

"This is your night, Cinderella," Brad whispered as they approached the crowded room. When Jo slipped her arm into his, he moved it away saying, "You don't need me in this dream; you don't need anybody." Jo searched his face for his meaning; Brad winked, whispering, "Go get 'em."

Jo smiled, turned and strolled boldly into the room thinking, *Cinderella my ass! I'm Annie Oakley tonight.*

Jo's eyes glanced around the room, noticing the shock register on the guests' faces. The room was divided into two sections. Groups of women were sitting around tables throughout the huge hall. Their eyes rose to meet her, some smiling graciously, some paling at her entrance. Jo nodded and waved, but her eyes left them, wandering across the room to the crowded bar. It was busy with the men of the industry, clapping each other on the back, exchanging horse stories. She stood very still, waiting for the word of her arrival to spread around the bar. As it did, their conversations halted. She had their full attention.

Jo walked straight toward the bar, notifying the room by her movements that she was there as a trainer and owner, not just Brad's date. Jo Martin walked toward her peer group of horse breeders, her gown rustling lightly with her steps.

As Jo approached the bar, she noticed several men nudge each other. Some cleared their throats, while other ordered fresh drinks. Jo greeted them, saying, "Hello Bob, Jeff, Harry." She flipped off other names as though they were in the practice of seeing each other daily. The men nodded, smiles coming to their faces. She took them all in, sweeping her hand dramatically. "It's good to see all of you again." They moved back, giving her access to the bar.

Harry Krane broke through the silence. "Is that you, Jo?" he asked, a grin covering his wrinkled face. "You've certainly changed these past two years." A slow mutter of agreement ran through the crowd.

Jo talked lightly with the men, accepting their compliments and courtesies. She spotted Sam Randolph circling from the end of the bar, his face set in silent fury. He looked older than a man in his fifties. "Why, it's Jo Martin," he said, breaking through the circle of men drawn around her. "What a surprise to see you here." His breath carried the aroma of strong whisky, a half-drained drink still in his thick hand. "I thought you'd be home raising a house full of brats by now." His eyes glared at her.

Jo accepted a glass of white wine from the bartender. She sipped it casually, organizing her words. Jo lifted her eyes to meet his, saying, "Sam Randolph, are you still involved with horses? I thought you'd be home in your rocking chair by now." A ripple of laughter surrounded her. The men licked their lips, excited for the next wave of conversation to hit.

Sam shifted his weight, looking more boxer than trainer. "The only rocking chair I sit in is the one behind my horses. My racing bike is my home, despite what some people have tried to do about it."

Jo watched as his eyes left hers and roamed around his circle of peers. He staggered slightly, silent testimony to his drunkenness. Jo caught the other drivers' disgusted looks, saw them move away from him. Sam turned his eyes back toward her. "So now you're all grown up." He motioned with his hand up and down her body. "What do you do with yourself now that you're," he staggered again, "all grown up?"

Jo smiled sweetly, hiding her disgust. "I train, Sam. I have a barn full of horses to care for. Remember that stallion you drove into the rail? I've bred him."

Sam's swaying motioned stopped, his bloodshot eyes narrowed, his arms moving up as if ready to punch her. The drink sloshed out of the glass forcing Jo to step back to save her gown. He sneered and laughed sadistically before saying, "You bred that piece of dog meat? You're even dumber that I thought."

Jo lifted her chin and moved toward him. She reached up and took the glass of whisky from his hands, her eyes revealing her hatred. She slid both his and her drink onto the bar. Jo lowered the pitch of her voice, making it more threatening; "Listen closely, old man."

The men leaned in, their eyes riveted on the two competitors, as if they were a stallion and filly heading into the home stretch. They were evaluating the two competitors before them, subconsciously making predications on who would win this round. They watched, curious to see if Jo would choke up and break stride.

"Are you sober enough to handle a wager?" she asked.

Sam wasn't confused. He knew she was about to challenge him in a bet between horse people. "I don't have to be sober to know I can beat you and any piece of dog meat you show up with," he growled back.

Jo placed her hands on her hips and leaned forward, inches away from his face. She announced for all to hear, "I'll bet you the token hundred dollars that my filly, sired by the horse you maimed, will take any horse you drive in the York Fair."

Jo heard the excited reaction of the men around her. This was a group of gamblers, who lived for the game, horseflesh against odds, drivers against time clocks. The race, the contest, was their lifeblood. These men didn't gamble for money. Horse people increased their worth by having the fastest horse. Their own pedigree was tied to their horses' track records.

Sam Randolph had been backed into a corner. "I'll beat you," he hissed through tobacco stained teeth. "Just like I always beat you."

Jo drew in her breath and shook her head empathetically. "No, Sam," she countered back. "Not like you did last time. I'm demanding a fair race, horseflesh against horseflesh. You know what I mean—no boxed-in conspiracies, no driving off the track. Just straight away stretches. I'll even take the air in my horse's face. Just give me a fair chance, and you'll end up eating my dust."

Sam squared his shoulder. She'd threatened not only him, but also all the drivers who'd acted like a gang, boxing her in. Jo turned to include them. "I don't want any special treatment because I'm a woman. I just want a fair shot for both me and my filly."

Harry Krane stepped up in front of Sam. "Okay, Jo," he said softly, "that's fair. No special treatment, either to help you or hinder you. If you've got guts enough to drive against us again, we're ready to treat you the same as any driver. We'll just forget you're a woman."

Jo reached out and shook Harry's hand. "That's a deal," she contracted. Several other drivers shook her hand, pledging their acceptance.

Sam Randolph pushed his way back to the center. He grabbed her hand, squeezing it with all his power. "It's a bet!" he bellowed. Then he turned and walked out the door. Sam Randolph had lost the first round in the race.

"I hope he doesn't hold his reins as tightly as he did my hand," Jo kidded, as she wiggled the reddened fingers to bring back the blood flow. The men erupted into laughter.

The room settled into a comfortable mood. The group slipped into the discussion of times, horseflesh and techniques. Jo drank in all the scuttlebutt concerning up-and-coming pacers. She answered questions about her horses, proudly announcing that she'd bred her mares to the stallion.

"You must be very confident in the ability of your filly," Harry Krane said, watching her closely. "You're betting your future on that horse."

"My filly is going to win that race," Jo announced with a confident smile.

"What do you know?" he answered. "You sound just like your dad. You sure don't look like him, though." The men laughed. Jo smiled, knowing the isolation she'd endured was now over. Her peers finally accepted her, and it felt wonderful. Time passed quickly, and it was almost ten before she spotted Brad talking with one of the owners. She excused herself and walked over.

Jo saw Brad's face break into a smile as he watched her cross the room toward him. He was talking with Fred Herman, who owned a horse farm a few miles up the road from hers. He'd been a good friend of her dad's. They both welcomed Jo, the man saying, "Your dad would have been proud of you. I'd wager that everyone in this room will be rooting for you when you race Sam Randolph." He nudged Brad, adding, "I can't wait to see it; how about you, Brad?'"

"I'd like nothing more than to see it, but I might not be here in September," Brad answered, his drawl suddenly thicker. He turned to look at Jo and saw her horrified expression. "Doc notified me today; he's putting his practice up for sale. The advertisement will be run in all the veterinary journals."

Jo felt like she'd been punched in the stomach, she couldn't breathe. Fred Herman sensed the depth of her shock so he said, "We all hope you'll buy it; you're one hell of a horse vet." He turned to Jo, adding, "Brad noticed my stallion was having slight, neurological problems. Turns out, he had EPM disease, caused by parasites carried by opossum. Seems we had an infestation of opossum in the rafters of our barn—never noticed it. Sneaky fellows could have infected all my horses. Brad gave me medication to cure my horse, and I called in the exterminators."

"Opossums are always a threat to horses in the South, one of the first things we check for," Brad answered. He looked back at Jo while saying, "I'd love to stay. You can't imagine how much, but I don't have that kind of money yet."

Fred shook his head, almost as if he was speaking for the stricken woman beside him, "What about the banks? You're a sure bet for success. You'd repay them in a couple of years."

Brad shook his head signaling no. "I'm up to my ears in debt from school. They're not going to lend me any more. I need some time to pay back what I owe before I can invest in a practice this big. It hits me a couple of years too early," he admitted.

Fred urged on, "What about your parents or relatives?"

Brad squared his shoulders. "Sorry, no help there. I only have my uncle left, and he's got his own sons to educate. No, he's done enough for me already. I'm on my own, but thanks." Brad turned to Jo adding, "I wish it could be different."

Jo heard the words from Brad's lips, those lips she had kissed so gently. He had never told her how all alone he was. She felt the pain for his loneliness, sorrow for his lack of roots; she wanted to reach out to him. They were both the same; they had no parents. Jo checked the tears that were brimming in her eyes, fearing that he would mistake her yearning love for pity. "Excuse me, do you know where the powder room is, Mr. Herman?" she asked turning from Brad just in time to hide the tear that slipped down her cheek.

"Let me show you the way," Mr. Herman answered, placing his hand under her elbow and ushering her away from Brad. They walked slowly, Mr. Herman giving her time to breathe in and gain control. "I'm sorry, Jo. I can see this upsets you."

"It does, more than you know," Jo answered honestly. "Maybe he'll find a way," she said hopefully, looking up into Mr. Herman's eyes.

"I don't want you to get your hopes up," Mr. Herman answered. "You have enough on your plate with the race. This comes at a bad time for both of you."

"It couldn't come at a worse time," Jo answered. "Please don't mention this to anyone."

"Your dad was my good friend. Trust me, my lips are sealed," he promised.

After a visit to the powder room, Jo walked out the French doors following the lighted path winding around the formal gardens. Several couples were out admiring the beauty of the flowers and shrubs, so Jo nodded as she passed them. In a far corner, she spotted a secluded iron bench. She walked over and sat down, grateful for the privacy. Once alone, she let her shoulders drop, the devastation of Brad's news hitting her full force. She was sad and heartbroken. Even the distant neighs of the magnificent horses didn't comfort her. *Only Brad can do that now*, she thought.

Jo took off her high heels and stood up; it was so simple. There was only one thing she wanted, and that was Brad. Barefoot, she moved quickly along the path back toward the mansion, thinking *I can be with him now. I can't waste one more minute.*

Brad was standing by the French doors, waiting for her. "Brad, "she said softly, "Can we leave now?"

Brad nodded saying, "Had enough?" His mouth twitched into a grin when he spotted the silver heels in her hand. "Get your glass slippers on and we'll go home, Cinderella."

They walked, side by side, not touching each other, lest the other departing guests take notice. Jo settled in the seat and took a deep breath, as Brad walked around the car and slid in behind the wheel. As he drove out the long drive, Brad spoke the first words. "You were wonderful tonight. I was so proud of you."

"Why, didn't you tell me about Doc's call before we came here?" she asked.

"That wouldn't have been fair to you, Jo. You had enough on your plate, facing Sam Randolph and all the other drivers. This was a very important night for you, and you handled it perfectly," Brad said.

"Brad, can we talk about Doc's call now?" she asked studying him closely.

"No, Jo. Please, not tonight. Do me a favor," he said turning to smile at her. "Tell me everything that went on at the bar. I heard several versions, and I want to hear about it straight from the horse's mouth."

"Who told you about it?" she asked, forcing herself to honor his request.

"I won't tell you until you tell me the true story." he answered, reaching up to undo his bow tie. He seemed to relax.

The ride home passed quickly while she told him all the details and he relayed the reactions of the men. When his car wheels turned into her driveway, she sighed happily. She had won the first round of the race. Now she looked forward to holding Brad in her arms and hopefully winning him.

They walked hand-in-hand toward her house. She opened the front door, expecting him to walk in after her. He didn't. Jo panicked and walked back outside. She found Brad out on the driveway, squatting down and patting Rowdy.

"I don't want to share you anymore tonight," she said in her sexiest voice, "not even with Rowdy."

Brad stood up slowly and turned toward her. "It's over Jo. Let's end it with this party, you dressed in that beautiful gown, me in a tux. It seems the perfect ending."

"What?" Jo gasped. "No, Brad. Let's spend each minute we have with each other."

"Jo, I can't. Every time I'm with you, I fall deeper in love with you. Can't you see that?" he admitted. His fingers ran through his hair, as if trying to clear his thinking. "It won't work; can't work. You have your own future. You've worked too hard to spend these next weeks throwing it away for more time with me. Now's your time to concentrate on training Little Girl. You have to go for it. Don't complicate your life with me."

Jo let the tears she'd held back run freely, "I love you Brad. I truly love you," she sobbed, grabbing his arms.

Brad reached down and took her face in his hands, whipping away her tears. "I know, Jo. Even you can't hide that from showing in your big, brown eyes, but that's why we've both got to stop seeing each other. I can't stay here much longer. Doc's practice will be snapped up in no time, Jo. If you were any other woman, I'd take you with me. I'm going to make a good living someday, just not right now. Fate has the timing all messed up."

Jo gasped for air, slowed her sobs, pleading, "Brad, ask me. I'll go with you. I don't have so much here, just a horse that might not even win. Brad, what future do I have without you?"

Brad dropped his hands from her face. "Don't you dare do this to me. I won't spend the rest of my life thinking of all you gave up for me. Every time you'd watch a race or see me work with a horse, you'd think of your home, your stallion, your pregnant mares and the filly you never got to prove a winner. Don't you do this to me."

Brad stepped away from her, his determination obvious. He ran his fingers through his hair again, then added, "Don't make me give up all my plans and dreams. I'm a vet, a good vet. Right now, that's all I have. Don't make it seem unimportant. I've worked too hard for it. I have a future to concentrate on—so do you. They can't be together; it's time we face it."

"Brad," she whispered, unable to fight the sobbing as he walked away. "Brad, please," she gasped as he pulled out the drive.

Brad took one last look in his rear view window, his own tears streaming down his face. He saw Jo collapse to her knees on the driveway, her hands covering her sobbing face, her small body surrounded by a pool of turquoise fabric, the moonlight revealing the white cleavage of her perfect breasts. He felt an ache in his heart, sensed sorrow surge through his veins poisoning his happiness.

Eleven

Jo was a survivor; she'd endured many tragedies. When Jo was twelve, her mother died of cancer. She'd gone on, taking over the duties of the house, burying her grief in work. At twenty-one, her lover abandoned her. She'd grown bitter but survived. At twenty-four, Jo's first horserace resulted in a lame stallion. Though distraught, she'd gone on. Her dad's death came close on the heels of the race. His death was horrific, but she'd honored her pop's last request by going on. At twenty-six, Jo had listened as her own stallion's heartbeat stopped. She'd gone on.

The loss of Brad was a completely different case, one she couldn't handle. The man she loved was still alive, living in the same town, working with horses, socializing with her peers, and wanting her as much as she wanted him. All her methods of survival didn't work. Brad's loss was devastating.

Jo wandered through the first three days in a fog. Brad had explained that Jo's dreams for her horse farm made it impossible for them to be together. Little Girl was the only animal capable of making the dreams come true. As a result, Jo began resenting the filly, training Little Girl with a vengeance. Little Girl, however, seemed undaunted by the challenge. The more Jo pushed her, the more the filly gave. With each flip of the reins, Little Girl ran faster. With each trip around the track, Little Girl was anxious for more. On the third day, as Jo brushed her exhausted horse, Little Girl nudged her. Tears began rolling down Jo's cheeks. She leaned forward, whispering into the animal's ear, "I know, Little Girl. You're still here and you'll do anything I ask of you. I do love you. We're so much alike, both stubborn as hell."

Little Girl moved her big head up and down as if agreeing, and the movement shocked Jo. She'd never allowed herself to feel connected to this small filly. Jupiter, her big stallion, had been her dream horse. Jo stepped back and looked into Little Girl's big, brown eyes. "Are you my dream girl?" she asked tilting her head. Little Girl nodded and nudged Jo with her soft nose. Jo dropped the brush and reached for the bag of barbecued potato chips. She ripped it open and held it while Little Girl devoured the contents of the bag. The old thrill for the race ran up Jo's spine. "You are my wonder horse, aren't you? No one expects us to win."

Nanny sensed the new energy in both her horse and guardian human. The goat moved up and nudged Jo, demanding recognition. "I see you, Nanny. You're there for me too, aren't you?" The goat let out a loud, bleating sound, which sounded like "Maa Maa." Jo threw back her head and laughed.

As Jo cared for her animals, she realized that Brad had been right. She couldn't abandon her dream. She needed to run the best race she could with Little Girl. If she didn't, she'd never forgive herself or Brad. She walked out and looked across the field. Her pregnant mares neighed and Rowdy ran up to snort his affection. "This farm is my life," she said breathing in deeply. "This is my home."

During the days that followed, Jo's work fulfilled her. At night, however, Jo had problems. She was exhausted, haunted by thoughts of Brad. The kitchen seemed larger and lonelier. The empty chairs around the oak table reminded her that Brad was gone. She ate standing up, listening to the sweet songs from the canary.

When the evening light faded, Jo's living room evoked misty memories. She thought of Brad carrying her in his arms or him running naked through her house. She pictured him standing in his black tuxedo, staring at her with surprise and desire.

The bedroom was the most painful spot for Jo. The soft bed seemed to bring his aroma back to her, and she lay awake reliving the memory of his hands across her body, the taste of his skin, the thrill of becoming one with the man she now knew she loved. Jo couldn't bear the bedroom. She avoided it and all its memories. Jo took to sleeping in the barn where her animals and their love surrounded her.

Ruben noticed the changes and he looked depressed. Feeling she let him down, Jo seldom talked to him. The farm developed a mood of obsession, Little Girl and the race being all that mattered. Everything else seemed to wither in the intense heat of August.

Time lost all significance. Only the daily notations made in the filly's training logbook reflected its passing. Over a month went by before Jo flipped the pages forward and realized only three more weeks remained until the race.

Jo closed the book and walked outside into the blaring sun. She felt weak and mentally exhausted. She climbed up to rest on the rail of the fence. All her life, it had been her favorite place to sit, but even it reminded her of the first day she'd met Brad. She reached down and unbuttoned her jeans. They felt tight around her waist. Everything bothered her now. She decided she was just tense.

Jo heard the sound of the hay truck entering her drive. She climbed down and struggled to zip up her jeans. "No time to relax," she thought as she sucked in her stomach. "More work's here."

Jo noticed a teenage friend of Mack's was driving. The freckled face of Billy smiled at her, as he proudly backed the large truck toward the barn. Sitting next to him, she spotted the slouching form of Mack. Jo dusted off her hands, unconsciously trying to shake off the bad memories Mack had caused. It didn't work, Jo found herself staring angrily at the uncomfortable boy.

Billy swung out of the truck, thrilled that he'd parked it successfully on the first try. "Hi, Jo," he yelled casually. "Bet you're surprised to see us. We're the new delivery boys for the hay farm. Some job, huh?" He thrust a clipboard in her direction, "Can't blame Mack for quitting. We make a lot more money delivering hay. You gotta sign the invoice," he instructed extending it again.

Jo's eyes watched Mack move to the back of the truck, where he began shoving off bales of hay. She stared, as the pile of bales grew larger. Jo ripped the clipboard out of Billy's hands. "So," she said loudly, "Mack told you he quit, did he?" she lifted her eyes to watch Mack's face turn red.

"Can't blame him," Billy continued, sensing her anger. "We get to meet all kinds of people on this job. We deliver to lots of horse farms, and people talk to us. Why, just yesterday Mr. Randolph, you know him, that trainer at Fairview Farms. He talked to us for near half an hour. You know he holds the record at the York Fairgrounds."

Jo's hand stopped signing the paper. She could feel the fear creeping down her spine. She leaned forward asking, "Just what did Mr. Randolph, have to say?"

Billy continued, thinking he'd impressed her. The drivers of delivery trucks were often used to obtain the quickest and most accurate information about what was happening on other farms and how their competitors' horses were doing. They were also used to send messages.

"He said he's gonna race you in September. I guess he knew Mack worked for you a while back. He must be a friend, huh? He wanted to know how you were doing in your training. Mack couldn't believe you were gonna race him. Mack told him the only horse you had left was Little Girl. We figured he'd ease up on you and give you a break. He sent you a message, *Don't worry. Don't push your luck. Racing might prove too much for your Little Girl.*" Billy smiled, delighted to bring the message. It seemed to make him feel like an important link in the underground of horse racing.

Jo's eyes grew wide with anger. She pictured Sam Randolph squeezing every fact he could from these naive and trusting teenagers. She could picture the scenario, Mack feeling important with inside information on Jo's horses. His ego, no doubt, was inflated by the interest of the famous driver. Jo shuddered to think what else Sam Randolph had managed to find out about her farm.

Jo took in a deep breath and looked down to sign the invoice. Her hand stopped a moment as she was thinking—*whatever happens next is going to spread like wildfire.* She looked up and watched Mack. He was done delivering the bails of hay but he'd jumped off the truck and started carrying one to her barn.

"What ya doing?" Billy asked. "All we have to do is deliver the hay."

"Not here," Mack said. "It's the least I can do for Jo."

Billy looked back at Jo. "We're not supposed to bring the hay into the barn."

Jo smiled saying, "Not even for a look at the horse that's gonna beat Sam Randolph's?"

"Wait, I'll help Mack," Billy said as he handed Jo the receipt.

"I can't believe that's the same horse," Mack said as the three stood looking at Little Girl."

"That's her," Jo said suddenly feeling motherly toward Mack. "She was a diamond in the rough, just like you, Mack." She put her hand on the teen's shoulder.

"I never told you how sorry I was about that day," Mack admitted.

"You don't have to feel sorry. You got a better job," Billy said enthusiastically.

"That's right," Jo said winking at Mack. "We all need to move on."

"How come she's not skittish anymore," Billy said grinning.

"She has her own Nanny," Jo said, pointing to the goat that was chewing on a piece of wood she'd found in the hay.

"That's weird," Billy added.

"It works. Little Girl's times are amazing. She's gonna win that race," Jo said confidently.

Jo waved at the truck as it pulled out. Mack waved through the open window, a look of relief on his face. Jo spotted Ruben and walked over to him. She placed a hand on his arm and said, "The hay's been stacked in the barn. Mack and Billy did it."

"Mack?" he said amazed.

"He's sorry. Many things are over and done with. It's time to move on; we've a race to win," Jo said smiling up at Ruben. "It's gonna be a good year for all of us."

Ruben looked at Jo and said, "Good!" Then he smiled.

Jo carried her bedroll and blankets up to her farmhouse, thinking *sleeping in the barn is ridiculous.*

Jo walked through her house, her hands running over her favorite things. I'm gonna have a good life here," she said, as she walked in the kitchen, suddenly craving a slice of liverwurst. She pushed things around in the refrigerator looking for the slices she'd bought a few days ago while in the deli. "Can't remember the last time I ate liverwurst. Maybe ten years ago when Dad dared me to try it."

Jo grabbed it, thrilled. She opened the package and picked up one piece with her fingers. Returning the rest, she casually walked around the kitchen, watering her plants and listening to her singing canary. She ate the liverwurst, as if it were a candy bar. "Delicious," she said smacking her lips. "Now all I need is a hot shower with the water full force. My shoulders ache."

Jo stepped into her shower and sighed. The force of the water felt wonderful on her shoulders. Aghast, she turned and jumped backwards. The water hurt her breasts. She messaged them, realizing that they were swollen and tender. *It must be that time of the month,* she thought.

By the time Jo stepped out of the shower, she was relaxed. She pulled her robe around her and walked outside the house. Jo stared out at the meadow toward the barn. She was glad that she'd been kind to Mack. She could have really embarrassed him in front of Billy. "He's just a kid," Jo thought. "I don't want to hurt his pride."

Jo sat on the porch glider thinking, *Pride? Is that what keeps me from running to Brad? Is that why I sit alone?* She ran her hand through her long, wet hair. Again, she thought back to the scene of the last time they were together.

"Do you want me to spend my life thinking of all you had to give up just to be with me?" Brad had yelled. Tears filled her eyes.

Jo spotted Rowdy coming up from the pond, another frog wiggling its legs in his mouth. Jo stood up and walked down the porch steps calling her dog, eager to have something that belonged to her. Rowdy trotted over, proudly plopping down his struggling catch. Jo stared blankly as Rowdy started rolling over on the smashed frog. The familiar sight suddenly nauseated her. Jo turned and ran into the bathroom, holding her hands over her mouth. Jo Martin was sick to her stomach.

Jo doused her face with water. She'd been vomiting for nearly fifteen minutes and it left her weak. She sat down on the edge of the bathtub, wiping her face with a wet washcloth. "Oh great," she sighed. "All I need is the flu." She pulled the robe tighter around her. It wasn't as comfortable as it used to be; nothing was.

Deep in her subconscious the facts began adding up. "Oh, no!" she screamed. "I might be pregnant." Her hands examined her own body, as though checking a strange patient's form. Her eyes noticed each bodily change, and her heart raced faster. She felt another wave of nausea come over her and reacted just in time. Jo was ill with her first recognized bout of morning sickness.

Jo lay across the bed, shaking and exhausted. Her head throbbed as she tried to check dates in her mind. She'd been so busy with the farm work, she hadn't noticed the feminine details of her own life. Jo realized that she had completely overlooked the obvious.

Jo's hands reached subconsciously to her stomach. They rested there, as though protecting some promise yet unconfirmed. A small smile came to her lips. "You stupid fool," she whispered to herself. "You never even thought of the possibility." Her smile widened. Although it didn't make sense, a strange calm came over her. Suddenly, the memories the room held were tender, beautiful moments to be recalled, like that first night, when she'd given up waiting for Brad, the lightening while he had made love to her. "That was the night," she whispered. "You were conceived that night." She laughed, "I'm glad." She fell into a deep, relaxed sleep, no longer bothered by lying in the big bed they had shared.

Twelve

The sound of the little bell brought memories of the last time Jo had visited the dress shop. Tears welled up as she stepped inside. Mrs. Van Order's smile faded as she studied the young woman heading toward her. The older woman's eyes showed compassion, and Jo walked straight to her open arms. Mrs. Van Order held her, until she whispered, "Give me one minute, and then we'll leave this place."

Mrs. Van Order walked into the back room. When she returned, her pocketbook was slung over her shoulder. "I completely forgot we had a luncheon date," she said winking. "Ethel will watch the shop for a few hours."

"Thank you," Jo whispered, as she was ushered out of the shop.

"Nonsense. I've wanted to take you to lunch. I heard about a delightful restaurant in York, The Roosevelt Tavern. It's supposed to have great crab cakes and desserts," she smiled, adding "and no one knows us in York."

"Thank you," Jo repeated.

"When is the baby due?" Mrs. Van Order asked as she drove out of town.

"How did you know? Do I already show?" Jo asked, horrified.

"Dearie. I've been in the clothing business all my life. I can spot when one of my clients gains five pounds. I know before they do that they need to move up a size," Mrs. Van Order assured her.

"I just came from the doctor's office. The baby is due in April. That's foaling season; can you believe it?" Jo said shrugging at the irony.

"Does Brad know?" Mrs. Van Order asked.

"How do you know his name?" Jo inquired.

"I've heard all about you showing up in that beautiful gown, looking like a vision from Vogue. Also heard you were accompanied by a handsome vet named Brad," Mrs. Van Order explained.

"No, he doesn't know. I came straight to your shop from the doctor's office," Jo admitted, still shaken.

"Good. You live in a man's world, but I don't think you've figured out that we women only let them think they're in charge," Mrs. Van Order explained. Jo looked up, hanging on her every word. "You have to handle them with a light touch, the same touch you use holding your reins. If you hold on too tightly, they'll rear up and head in the wrong direction."

They settled into leather seats and looked around the elegant restaurant. "This is lovely, isn't it?" Mrs. Van Order remarked. "Let's order and then we'll get down to work."

"I can't believe I'm pregnant," Jo said shaking her head, "and I'm going to be a mother?"

"Your mother was a natural," Mrs. Van Order announced. "You will be too. Do you remember how much fun you two had with each other?"

"Yes, I do," Jo said thinking back. "I haven't thought about that for years. It was too painful after she died, but you're right. She was a wonderful mom."

"And a great friend to me," Mrs. Van Order stated.

"Should I tell Brad?" Jo asked. "He's leaving town."

"I heard Doc is selling his practice, so why is he leaving?" Mrs. Van Order asked.

Jo explained why Brad was leaving and how much they loved each other. Mrs. Van Order listened, a gentle look of concern on her face. Jo ended her story with a deep sigh and shrug, "It's hopeless. I don't want him to know about the baby. I won't use the baby to trap him into marriage."

"Of course you won't," Mrs. Van Order agreed, "but you won't have to. From what you've told me, the solution is simple."

"Solution? There's a solution?" Jo asked, hopefully.

"Of course. You only have two barriers preventing it: money and two different dreams. When you think about it," Mrs. Van Order said slowly, her fingers tapping lightly on her ice tea glass, "your dreams aren't different."

Jo saw the spark come into the older woman's blue eyes. Mrs. Van Order continued, "Brad's been living with an uncle who had his own sons. It must have been difficult being the one kid who didn't belong, like being a visitor who stayed too long. That's why having a home of his own is so important to him, and that's why he understands how much your farm means to you. You could never leave Hobby Hill Farm."

"That makes sense. You should see him looking out over my pastures. He understands why I'm rooted to my farm," Jo added.

"Your dream is to secure the future of your home. In truth, you both have the same dream," Mrs. Van Order explained. "The one barrier is money."

"I'm so broke that I'm going to ask the bank for a loan. I've been getting all my accounts ready for them to go over. I need to hire help now that I can't lift heavy things, and there is a long list of things I need for the race." Jo explained.

"Can your horse win that race?" Mrs. Van Order asked. "I mean it, no pipe dreams. Can your horse win?"

Jo looked up and suddenly her face radiated confidence. "My horse is going to win that race," Jo answered with confidence. "The doctor said I can train and drive in the race since it's only three weeks away. I just have to stop lifting anything heavy."

"Then you can win more than the race. Do everything possible to ensure that victory and make your vet part of it all. Don't go to the bank; ask him for the money. Tell him that you'll make him part owner of your horse. The man doesn't want handouts; he wants to be part of something. Make that possible," Mrs. Van Order suggested.

"What if he doesn't want to bet his money on my horse?" Jo asked.

"Then let him go. He doesn't love you as much as he says he does. He'll never know how much he's losing," Mrs. Van Order explained. "In my opinion, no woman needs to live with a martyr who marries her out of obligation. Life's too short. You and your child don't need that."

"My child," Jo said sliding her hands over her stomach. "You're right. We don't need that. We're going to have a great life with or without Brad."

"Can I be the grandma?" Mrs. Van Order asked sheepishly. "I only have one grandchild and she lives in Europe. I'd love to be your baby's surrogate grandma."

Tears welled up in Jo's eyes. "Yes, please. I'm sure mom would've suggested that. I have mom's rocking chair in my old bedroom. You can sit and rock the baby and I'll cook you dinner."

"Yes and maybe Brad will be there," Mrs. Van Order suggested.

"Ruben must be the grandpa," Jo said smiling. "He'd be the natural choice. Maybe this will put a smile on his face."

"Does he still work at your farm? I grew up with Ruben," Mrs. Van Order said, smiling shyly. "He was my first love."

"Ruben? He's so quiet that I can't see you two together," Jo added.

"He is the best listener I've ever known," Mrs. Van Order explained.

"What happened to you two?"

"I married my second love," she shrugged. "He's been dead for over five years. Call me Audrey," Mrs. Van Order suggested, "until the baby's born. Then I'm Grandma."

Jo walked into her farmhouse loaded down with two pairs of roomy jeans, three big tee shirts and one blouse. Her other arm held a grocery bag of fruits, vegetables and vitamins.

After dumping the packages, Jo looked around her farmhouse, thinking *this is a beautiful place to raise my child.* Jo walked straight to the door of her old bedroom. She opened it slowly, almost afraid to disturb sleeping, childhood memories. It was dusty and dark, the shades closed. Jo lifted the blinds and opened the windows. The fresh air rushed in, as if it had been waiting outside for this moment.

Pictures covered the walls, remnants of days gone by. Her single bed was covered with stuffed animals and other memorabilia. Jo had avoided this room, refusing to dwell on the past. Now pregnant, she allowed herself to look back at her own childhood, to remember those happy days growing up in this house on her farm.

Jo walked over to her bed, a melancholy coming over her. She sat on the edge, picking up a well-worn stuffed bunny. Her hands caressed the faded animal, as she thought of all the nights that she'd held it tightly in her arms. "I forgot how magical it can be when you're a child." Her eyes roamed around the room, taking in the scattered pictures. In one, she was a little girl dressed for Halloween; in another, she was a cheerleader, waving her pompoms at a high school game, and then she was standing in cap and gown clutching her college diploma.

Jo smiled, as she touched her tummy. "This is your room, young'un. You're going to love it," she promised.

Brad was placing medications in his jeep when his phone rang. He was tired, lack of sleep draining him. He'd lost interest in both his work and his life in Hanover. He wanted to escape, to put as many miles as possible between Jo and him. The constant temptation to return to her farm was wearing him down. Brad reached over and grabbed the phone. "Yes," he grumbled, annoyed. His eyes narrowed when he heard the sweet voice on the other end. "Is that you, Jo?" he asked, his blue eyes closing to visualize the woman on the other end.

"Yes, Brad," Jo answered. "How many other women do you have calling you up?"

Brad's heartbeat jumped and he ran his fingers through his hair. "Oh, not that many," he answered, trying to meet her mood.

Jo pushed the phone closer to her ear, hungry for the sound of his voice. "I need your help," she continued, wetting her dry lips. "Little Girl's legs are swelling. Would you mind taking a look at them?" There's only three weeks left before the race. I don't want anything to give me trouble."

Brad felt like he'd been sucker punched. "Sure," he said, disappointed with this professional call. "I'm still your vet." He found himself wondering what she was wearing, and he shook his head in frustration.

"Brad," Jo continued carefully, "I hope you're more than just my vet. I hope you're still my friend."

He held his breath, half-afraid to answer. "Jo," he returned, "it'll be hard to just be your friend."

"No, it won't," Jo promised. "I won't seduce you if that's what you're afraid of."

"You never seduced me," Brad assured her. "Hell Jo, even the sound of your voice turns me on."

"Well, you'll have to get control over that because I need your friendship and advice. I'm going to exercise Little Girl for an hour. It's her light day. Her legs will be swollen even after one hour, and you'll see why I'm worried. Can you come over around three?"

"I'll be there," Brad answered, "but don't be wearing that damn turquoise dress. God, you looked beautiful in that thing."

"I'll be wearing jeans and a sweaty tee shirt. It's hot out," Jo laughed. "See, you'll be perfectly safe."

"I don't know. The words tee shirt, hot, and sweaty brings different images," Brad said laughing.

"Control yourself, buddy. I need your help," Jo warned.

"I'll be over in an hour," Brad promised.

Brad's jeep pulled into the driveway earlier than expected. He hadn't been able to stay away. Jo needed him and that was all that mattered. His eyes spotted her bathing the horse, the goat close by, nibbling on some grass. He stared, hungry to look at the woman he'd missed so much. Her golden hair was wet, the water running down her shirt, making it stick closely to her body. She turned causally and waved a friendly greeting. Brad's fingers formed into

a tight fist. She was beautiful in body and spirit. He wanted her—
he wanted to run to her and take her in his arms. He longed to
caress her, exploring all those delicious curves. He turned away,
trying to gain control over his emotions. "Life's just not fair," he
sighed bitterly.

Stepping out of the jeep, he took in a deep breath and remembered *I have to be just her friend; she needs me. That's all I can ever be, a
mere buddy to call on for help.* Brad walked slowly toward the woman,
his nerves on edge.

"You look like you're taking a bath along with Little Girl," he
said, as he settled on the fence rail.

"It's this blasted heat," Jo continued, running the sweat trough
over Little Girl's back. "I decided to douse myself with the water
first. Thought I'd have time to dry out before you got here. Her
eyes met his, sending shivers down his spine.

Brad looked away shrugging, "I hear friends don't try to change
each other. You're perfect any way you want to be. You sort of
look half-mermaid, half-cowgirl." A smile spread across his lips. He
relaxed, the first tense moments gone. He enjoyed being with her,
had missed her more than she'd ever know. "Where's Rowdy?"
he asked, looking around. "Is he mad at me? He hasn't bitten my
boots or wet down my tires yet."

Jo laughed, and shrugged, "He's not mad at you. It seems
Rowdy has found a girlfriend. Get this, Brad; the collie on the
next farm is in heat. Can you imagine? That's all I need—six, big,
hairy, brindle mutts with short, bowed legs. Ugh." She took her
equipment to the shed, still laughing.

Brad threw back his head and laughed warning, "Collies can
have up to ten pups. Let's hope her owner is keeping her safely

inside. Collie and mutt bull? They'd chase every car that goes by the farm, then try to chew the tires." It felt good to be back with Jo. He felt refreshed and more himself. "I hope you warned him about Rowdy."

"I did. I called them when I saw Rowdy cross the crest of the hill. You think that's funny, watch this," Jo said, pulling out a pail of barbecue potato chips. Little Girl's nose twitched in excitement. The horse thrust her nose into the pail and began chomping the crisp chips. "I've got a race horse that's addicted to barbecue chips. She downs almost twenty pounds a week. I gave up going to the Utz factory to get them. They send a truck to deliver them here like I'm some sort of restaurant. I think everything's neurotic around this farm. Look at the goat you saddled me with. It thinks it's a dog."

Brad continued his laughing. "Oh, Jo, you're too tolerant, much too tolerant."

Jo spoke, and he noticed the change in her tone, "I told you a long time ago that I don't want to break them of their individual spirits. I just respect them, and take what they give freely." Her eyes lifted to meet his and he knew she was talking about their relationship.

"I know that, Jo, and I thank you," Brad said looking at her. "You're certainly not a control freak. You accept everyone as they are."

Brad showed Jo how to apply the ointment to the filly's legs, and then he wrapped them in tight stall bandages. "Keep her in bandages whenever she's in the stall. Put lighter bandages on when she's working out on the track. You have to cut back on those chips, Little Girl. Too much salt. Try eating carrots or apples for your treat," Brad suggested near the filly's ear.

Brad patted Little Girl and walked out of the stall. "She looks good, Jo. He looked down and his eyes roamed over Jo's body. You both do. Seems you both filled out a little; you look great."

Jo blushed and said, "Thanks. I'm so nervous about the race that I keep eating." She looked up into his eyes adding, "I've nothing else to ease my tension."

Brad laughed. "Well, you needed to eat more; you have a glow about you now. You must be excited for the big race. What's Little Girl's time?"

"Oh no you don't," Jo said laughing. "You have to come find out for yourself. I'm running her tomorrow around nine. Can you come over? I need you to time her, give me your opinion and any tips that will help. I need some business advice, too. I know you'll tell me the truth."

They walked toward Brad's jeep. "Sure, I'll be happy to help you any way I can," Brad assured her.

They both stopped and watched Rowdy lifting his leg and peeing on Brad's tire. "Some things never change," Brad said smiling. Rowdy finished and quickly turned, heading for the barn. "Not even a nudge for a pet?" Brad said disappointed.

"He's going to spend the afternoon napping. From the snorts he makes, I think he's having sexual dreams," Jo said shaking her head.

"He's not the only one," Brad admitted as he climbed into his jeep.

Jo answered, "Don't I know? We're a group of frustrated lovers."

Brad closed the car door, needing to put a barrier between them. He sighed heavily and rolled his eyes.

Jo leaned through the open car window. She kissed the tip of one of her fingers and lightly pressed it on his warm lips. Brad reacted instinctively, parting his lips and running his tongue against her flesh. "Horses and syrup," he said, as his eyes roamed over her body again. "You still taste the same." He reached down and turned on the engine. "See you tomorrow at nine."

Thirteen

Jo stood beside her horse, her hand nervously twisting the reigns. The training cart was hitched up; the track gate open. All she needed was Brad. Jo looked down at her watch, 9:10. He was late, perhaps not even coming. She rubbed her hand over the horse's back. "Well, Little Girl," she said softly, "if he comes, it'll be up to you. You have to impress him, so he realizes we can win. Run for our lives, Little Girl."

Jo looked up as she heard Brad's jeep pull in her driveway. A shiver ran through her; the race was starting. Jo waved and situated herself into the training bike. She flicked her reins yelling, "Let's go, Little Girl."

Jo headed the filly toward the track as Brad walked through the field. She urged Little Girl into a steady jog, bringing the horse's body heat up. Little Girl's head lifted into the wind, her eyes bright with the work at hand.

Brad waved to Ruben as he crossed the field. The old man walked to his side, both of them keeping their eyes on the woman driving the filly around the track. "Nice to see you," Ruben said, his tone saying more than his words.

"I'm anxious to see how the horse does," Brad answered, hoping to put off the man's curiosity. Together they walked on, just the clop of Jo's pacing horse breaking their strained silence.

As Brad and Ruben pulled themselves up on the fence, Jo took in a deep breath. Her hands tightened on the reins, her own heart pounding with excitement. She circled close to them, calling out her warning, "Get ready. Set your stop watches." She passed them, deciding to go one more quarter before turning Little Girl the racing way.

Jo gave the horse the signal and turned her in a wide, half circle. The horse raised her head and flared her nostrils, as though smelling the challenge she had been given. Jo slapped the reins across the filly's back, urging her on. The race had begun.

The filly's hoofs pranced into a quick pace, her legs moving in rhythmic action. Jo could almost feel the stopwatches start. She pushed Little Girl harder, forcing the message of urgency through the reins to the horse. The horse reacted, going faster. When Jo circled the half-mile track, the amazed faces of Brad and Ruben confirmed that her time was good. She pushed on, the filly stretching forward into the wind. In the third quarter, the filly increased her pace, seeming to enjoy the speed Jo was allowing. The fences began to whirl past, and Jo's, heart pounded harder—the homestretch was at hand.

It was as though Jo was back on the fair track. She could almost hear the crowd shouting, almost hear the hoof beats of other horses. Jo's body reacted to the challenge. She urged Little Girl on faster into the stretch. The horse ran harder, increasing the speed. Jo held her breath, half-afraid the filly would break, going out of her pace into a full gallop. That would mean total failure. Still, Jo pushed the horse harder, counting on the breeding of her filly, counting that the instinct to pace would carry the young filly across the finish line.

The filly's eyes were wild with excitement, her body a sheet of perspiration. Little Girl held her form and crossed the finish line in a perfect pace. She had made the best run of her life, and Jo loved the little horse more now than ever before. They were both small, but they could both be winners. Jo released a deep breath, easing Little Girl into a slower jog, careful to bring her back to a gentle stop. Her eyes watched Brad carefully. He was checking times with Ruben, yelling enthusiastically. Their actions told Jo all she needed to know; her horse was fast. She had a chance.

Jo headed Little Girl over toward the men. "What's her time?" she yelled.

"Two minutes and twenty seconds for a mile. Do you believe it"? That little filly just did two-twenty and on this farm track!" Brad shouted, amazement showing in his eyes. "I can't believe it, Jo. That horse is a real winner."

"That's not half bad," Jo sighed, a thrill running through her. She slipped off the cart, steadying her shaking legs. "Ruben," she asked politely "Would you mind walking Little Girl until she blows out slowly. I need to talk to Brad."

Ruben smiled eagerly, "Let's go, Little Girl. I'll wash and take her back, too." Jo saw him smile, as he led the horse around the track. He hadn't seen Little Girl train in quite a while, as though he'd been afraid to watch, afraid of what he might see. His smile showed he had become a believer. Nanny bleated her maa maa toward the filly. Little Girl neighed and shook her head in return.

Jo laughed and then quickly reached out, grabbing onto the fence. She felt dizzy. The world seemed to whirl around her.

Brad jumped off the fence and took her in his arms. "Jo, are you all right?" he asked, pulling her closer to his own body.

Jo's ear pressed against Brad's chest; she heard the thick heart-beat and it centered her. He held her for a few minutes; his body reacted to her closeness and exposed his desire. Jo opened her eyes, realizing this contact was not going to be good. She stead-ied herself and reached for the fence, easing herself free from his hold. "I'm sorry, Brad." she said lifting one hand to her head. "In my rush to get the chores done, I forgot to eat anything. I'm light headed."

Brad watched her carefully, saying, "You work too hard. Come on, I'll cook breakfast while you rest. Ruben's got Little Girl. Besides, it's all I can do to keep myself from kissing you. Damn, Jo, you were magnificent."

"Don't ever apologize for wanting me," Jo said, as they walked toward the farmhouse. "I'd be apologizing all day long if we started that."

Brad laughed, grateful for her quick wit. "You sure don't mince words, do you, Jo."

"I'm becoming more like Ruben every day," Jo said. "I need a glass of milk and food."

"Since when did you start drinking milk?" Brad asked.

"Since the doctor told me to. He also told me to stop lifting anything heavy. Seems he's thinks I do too much," Jo admitted.

"You do," Brad said shaking his head. "Are you going to hire some help?"

"That's what I need to talk to you about," Jo said as they walked up the porch steps. "Can you really cook?"

"Sure can," Brad admitted. "I can sling hash with the best of them—worked in a little restaurant while in college. My specialty is breakfast. Get ready to watch the master," Brad warned.

Jo sank to the chair, grateful to sit on something that wasn't moving in circles. Leaning forward, she propped her head on her hands, as Brad opened her refrigerator. "You have actual food in here. Good stuff. I'm glad to see you're taking care of yourself," Brad said smiling. "I was afraid all you'd have was Little Girl's chips."

Jo laughed, relaxing. "No. I'm all about keeping both of us healthy. By the way, Little Girl is not impressed with carrots. Now apples, she can manage them."

"Drink this coffee while I start slinging," he said as he set her cup down.

"Slinging? Are you one of those cooks that make a mess?" Jo kidded.

"Of course," Brad said as he cracked eight eggs with obvious flare. "Tell me about the wreck you had with Sam Randolph. I notice you flinch every time you make the back turn."

"I do?" Jo said her eyes opening wide. "Oh no. I can't do that?"

"Don't worry; I can help you stop that. Tell me about the wreck, so we know what we're dealing with," Brad said, while turning on the stove and putting down the frying pan.

"Well, it was the result of a lot of factors. You see," Jo said, looking away as if searching her memory, "the other drivers were upset that a woman was racing against them. They realized that the stallion was a real threat because they'd watched him train for several days. Oh, Brad, he really was magnificent, such a strong pacer," she sighed. "They didn't want the track record broken by a woman driver." She watched Brad put the bacon into the frying pan and then slipped the toast into the toaster.

Go on," Brad said, before taking a sip of coffee and turning toward her.

"Some of the men told me to watch out. They were friends of our family and had heard some of the drivers plotting. Years ago, we could all move to the fairgrounds for a few weeks before the races. They let us train on the track. They don't let us do that anymore. No more room. They flattened rows of barns to make room for the UTZ Arena. Maybe that's good. Living that close, you watch each other's horses, learn their idiosyncrasies, hear all kinds of scuttlebutt. Drivers have fun trying to get in each other's heads. I'd learned about it in college, so I ignored it all. I was young and naive, had no idea how serious it was." Jo shrugged and took another long sip of coffee. The discussion was bringing back bad memories.

"Tell me, Jo. It's important," Brad urged.

"On the day of the race, they ganged up on me during the first half-mile, boxing me in. They were keeping me blocked behind, so I wouldn't set a new record. During the second half-mile, they pulled away, satisfied that I couldn't break it."

"I'm so sorry. That must have frustrated you," Brad surmised.

"Yes, but the accident wasn't caused by me taking chances. Sam Randolph caused the problem. Some say he was driving under the influence of alcohol, some say he just hates women because his wife ran off with another man. I don't know what made him do it, but on the last turn I was ahead. I was winning that race." Her eyes shone with pride until she looked down, her shoulders dropping.

"That's great. You pulled up from behind. Go on," Brad urged again.

"It was Sam Randolph and my horse. I was running ahead of him. He went crazy! He drove his bike into mine, our wheels caught, and my racing bike flipped over the track rail. The cart jerked the stallion to an immediate stop. The force injured his muscles and broke one bone. That's why he still limps. I ended up with a concussion and a few broken bones. They said I was lucky to be alive. The aluminum, racing bike landed on top of me. Needless to say, its chassis was bent and one wheel torn completely off. It was a bad accident."

"Jo," Brad said, his mouth opened in astonishment. "Why do you want to race again?"

"My dad had nightmares about it for days. Then one night, while I was still in the hospital, he died in his sleep, a heart attack. Dad died all alone, a broken and disappointed man," Jo said shaking her head.

"My God," Brad said as he turned away. He flipped the bacon slowly, grateful she couldn't see the tears in his eyes. "Go on," Brad encouraged.

"That's why I have to race again. Everyone blamed dad for encouraging me, a small-framed woman, to go into racing. They predicted I'd never race again because I'd been through too much. They said our farm had its once-in-a-lifetime horse."

Jo lifted her head, her eyes flashing. "They're wrong, Brad. I've got to prove my dad was right when he risked everything on his stallion and when he believed in my ability. The only way I have left is through Little Girl. This farm and its horses are my inheritance. I have to make it a success because it's all I have left."

Brad looked over at her, "You'll do it," he told her. "You're a great trainer and driver. I'll help you get past that twitch on the corner, but now you need a new racing bike? Do you have the money? Jo, you need lots of things to race."

Jo got up and walked to her desk, returning with her farm's accounting books and her list of things she needed. Brad filled their plates and served their food.

"I know. I've been working on the figures and they're not very good. I need all these things and don't have the money. I can go to the banks and ask for another loan, but I already owe them money. I've made every monthly payment on time. We're above water now because of the boarding mares, but there's no extra money."

Jo moved back to her seat and urged, "Look through the books. The loan will have to go through the approval process, which means they'll take it to the board. Most of them saw the wreck and subscribe to the theory that women don't belong on the race track. I'm scared they won't approve the loan, Brad. Once a bank refuses a loan, you might as well kiss your farm goodbye."

"Eat," Brad urged as he looked over her books. They ate in silence, Jo nervously watching and answering his questions. Finally he closed the book saying, "You've made some good decisions. Letting the farmer plant your far acreage in hay was a good way to use your land and get free feed. You could use some of the farm land to handle more mares?"

Yes," Jo said. "I've been trying to fence in new pastures for the spring fouls. Haven't gotten very far with all the training I've been doing. I need to hire some help for that, I guess," Jo admitted.

Brad shook his head and laughed. "You can't do it all. It has nothing to do with you being a woman. No one could."

"Brad, will you loan me the money? I believe Little Girl is going to win. Do you? "

Brad shook his head *yes* and smiled.

"How'd you like to be part owner of Little Girl?" Jo continued, encouraged by his nod. "I need five thousand dollars. See this list?" she asked, as she got back up and pointed to the paper on the table. "I need a new racing bike, and then I need to take Little Girl to the track the night before the race. Nanny and I will bunk in with her." She moved back to her seat and stabbed her fork into her eggs, giving Brad a chance to think about her offer. "I forgot," she continued. "I need racing silks; mine were cut off me in the hospital." She watched Brad's eyes close and his body shiver. It touched her.

"I also need to hire some help for Ruben, a farm hand to do all the heavy work." She sighed, "I'm talking too much; it's all there on that paper. It comes to about $5,000."

"I have saved some money," he said gently, aware of the pride she was burying to ask for money. A lump came to his throat as he realized that he'd never been asked for financial help. He'd always been the one who needed a handout. All his years of hard work were beginning to pay off. Suddenly he could provide for the woman he loved. "I can't think of anyone I'd rather invest in, Jo. You're a winner in my book," was his answer.

With those few words, Brad confirmed his belief in her dream. He not only loved her but had confidence she would win. She jumped out of her chair and ran around the table, plopping onto his lap, spreading light kisses over his face.

"Back woman," he yelled, laughing heartily. "You're driving me absolutely mad."

"Good," she whispered, in a teasing tone. "Give in."

Brad pulled back and looked into her eyes saying, "Sit over there, please Jo. We need to talk about some other things."

Jo froze and moved.

"I had a feeling you were still hoping for a future together. You are one stubborn woman," he said affectionately. "I would love nothing more. We'd have one great life together, wouldn't we?"

"Yes," Jo added, tempted to tell him about the baby.

"You're not the only one who was looking for a way for us to be together. I told Doc that I wanted to see you race and asked if he'd put off the ad. He agreed and asked if I was going to buy his practice. I told him 'No'. So after the race, it goes up for sale."

Jo shook her head and said, "I'm so sorry."

"It gets worse," Brad added. "Then he reminded me that I had signed a contract when I came here. For ten years, that contract will keep me from practicing veterinary medicine within a one hundred mile radius of Hanover."

"Oh no," Jo said, slumping in her chair.

"Yes, it's regular procedure. I never thought I'd meet you, Jo. Now I'm out of luck. We're both back to square one," Brad admitted.

He looked over at Jo and continued, "Honey, you have enough on your stubborn shoulders now. I'm worried about you racing, especially after I heard about that wreck. Besides that, I don't think there will be enough money to buy the practice. Is that what you were hoping for?"

Jo nodded and whispered, "Yes. I love you, Brad."

"I love you too, but we agreed it's over," Brad replied.

"What if Little Girl breaks the record? We could borrow money for you to buy the practice then. Think of the stud fees that we'll get once the stallion's bloodline is proven. We have four of his fouls coming. They will be worth a lot of money," Jo said enthusiastically.

"Do you hear yourself?" Brad said reaching over to hold her hand. "Just the fact that you get back out on the race track after that wreck is a miracle. Everyone will be impressed. Little Girl will give a good run; you don't even have to win to gain back everyone's respect. Now you're hell bent on breaking that record to help me out. Jo, you can't hope for all that; I don't want you to. I want you to train for one thing, a safe race to show them what you can do. That's all. You have to promise me that or I walk out right now. I don't want you putting yourself in any danger because of me."

Jo stared at him, numb. She'd almost told him about their baby. If she had, everything would be over. He'd stop her from racing all together.

"All right, she said sighing. "I'll run a safe race, but I'll pay you back. You're right, the banks will give me a loan after the race even if I don't win. I'll pay you back, I promise."

"No rush. I've got no plans for that money." He stood up and carried the dishes to the sink. "You have to clean up. I'll go to the bank. I have a favor though," he said.

"Anything," Jo said, trying to smile.

"There's another woman in my life, named Coco. I don't go anywhere without her." He watched as Jo's eyes opened wide. "She's my quarter horse. I'd like to bring her over here, so I can ride around your farm. I can't believe you don't have a horse you can actually ride."

Jo's relief was obvious. "In that case bring her over. I've got plenty of empty stalls. It was a cow farm, remember?"

"Yes I do. I figured I could stay here while you're bunking in at the fairground. I'll do the heavy work around here, plus I do hate those pop records. It's parade season and they practice every night."

Jo laughed, saying, "I don't leave for days. Want to move in early?"

Brad turned and stared at her. A slow, sexy smile came to his lips. "We could be friends with benefits, but that's all it will ever be. Can you handle that?" Brad asked seriously.

"I'll take what you offer. I'm not a control freak, remember?" Jo said.

His smile radiated, "I'll be back around five. Ruben will be gone by then. It's so hot that I think we both deserve a dip in that pond."

Fourteen

Jo stood on the front porch as Brad drove his jeep up from the barn. He stopped and leaned out the open window saying, "You better order all those things on your list."

"Do you have to leave right now?" Jo asked in her sexiest voice.

"We both have work to do," he warned. One hand raked through his hair, as if he might change his mind. He finally looked up, smiled and suggested, "Get to work; we have a race to win." He waved and pulled away.

"We do have a race to win," she said, as happy tears rolled down her cheeks. She looked down toward the barn and saw Ruben had finished washing Little Girl. *I need to tell Ruben what's going on*, she realized. *He's devoted his entire life to my family and this farm.* She brushed her tears away and walked toward the barn noting, *and I better get a grip on my emotions. This must be the rush of hormones the pamphlet talked about.*

Ruben was walking Little Girl and Nanny out to their pasture. Jo joined them. "I have good news," she said patting Little Girl as they walked. "Brad is going to lend me $5,000, so I can order what I need to race." Ruben didn't comment so Jo continued, "I'll spend the night before the race at the fairgrounds." They reached the pasture,

Ruben opened the gate and Little Girl and Nanny walked through. "Brad will help you out around the farm; he's going to bring his quarter horse here." Ruben was closing the gate. "He'll only be here part time because he still has the vet practice to handle."

Ruben turned to look at her, saying nothing. "I'm pregnant," she said, not knowing why. She watched as his eyebrows rose, his head jerked to one side and his hand rose to cover his mouth. "Tell me what you're thinking, Ruben" she asked.

Ruben sighed and shook his head, as if letting it all sink in. "I'm afraid he might leave," he finally admitted.

Jo walked toward Ruben, and he lifted his arms and wrapped them around her. She answered, "I am, too. He doesn't know about the baby. He wouldn't let me race if he knew." Ruben patted her back. "The doctor said it was all right, so don't worry about it, please." She stepped back and looked up at him. "If we break the track record, he'll be able to buy Doc's practice, but he told me not to even think about that."

Ruben shook his head and said, "Then he doesn't know you very well." They both laughed. "Are you going to be all right if he leaves?"

"Yes," we're all going to be all right, Jo said. "You'll be the Grandpa, and I already have a surrogate Grandma ready and waiting."

"I'll be a Grandpa?" Ruben said, his eyes tearing up.

"Audrey Van Order has agreed to be the Grandma. She was my mom's best friend, remember her?" She watched as Ruben's head jerked up and his eyes stared. "She told me you were her first love," Jo added. "Said you listened better than anyone she'd ever known."

Ruben dropped his gaze and chuckled.

"We'll all be all right," Jo said as they began to walk toward the barn. "Brad does love me."

"I know," Ruben answered, "and I like the man." He looked back at Jo, and asked, "When's the little one coming?"

"April, right in the middle of foaling season." They both laughed and shook their heads.

When Brad finally returned, his jeep was pulling a horse trailer. Both Jo and Ruben walked toward the barn, eager to see his horse. Brad opened the trailer and positioned the ramp. He led his horse out, announcing, "I'd like to introduce Miss Coco, the sweetest quarter horse you'll ever meet, bred from gentle stock." The horse followed Brad, looking thicker than any other mare on the farm. She was dark brown, with a splash of white forming a triangle on her forehead.

"She's a knockout," Jo said, letting Coco smell her hands. Ruben walked into the barn leading the way to Coco's new stall. Brad, Jo, and Coco followed. "I'd like to take her for a ride; want to join us?" Brad asked.

"How?" Jo asked.

"We'll ride double, with your arms around my waist," Brad explained. "It'll be sexy."

"You won't go fast; I can't get hurt before the race," Jo said automatically.

"You're not afraid to race at the fairgrounds, but you are afraid to ride horseback," Brad said laughing. "You are one crazy horse person. Don't worry, nothing will ever hurt you on my watch," he said, looking lovingly at Jo.

"Then count me in," Jo announced. "While you get saddled up, I'll go turn the oven off. The roast should be done. Pick me up at the house," Jo said in an excited tone.

She watched him riding up toward the house, a brown cowboy hat on his head. She laughed, thinking about all the books she'd read as a young girl. They were always books about horses, the hero always a cowboy. She stood on the porch, relishing being in love, happy, and pregnant with her first child.

"Give me your hand," Brad said, as he leaned down. Jo took a deep breath, and reached toward him. He lifted her up and swung her toward the back. She encircled her legs around Coco. "You've done this before, haven't you?" he asked.

"Of course," Jo admitted. "During my wild, college days." They both laughed as Jo reached her arms around his waist. She kissed his neck and then pressed her cheek against his back.

"Giddy up Coco," Brad said, flicking his reins. The three moseyed out toward the outer acreage of Jo's farmland.

Brad pulled up on the reins saying, "whoa Coco." They stopped on top of a large hill. He climbed down from the saddle and then eased Jo off into his waiting arms. They hugged looking out over the farmland. "It's beautiful here," Brad said. "Your land has gentle slopes, rich soil, streams and ponds. It's got everything you could want."

"Not everything," Jo said as she hugged Brad tighter.

"Who lives in that little spread over there?" Brad asked. "He's got some good looking quarter horses."

"That's Ruben's house. I think he fenced in around five acres for his own horses. He rides Gabriel to work, keeps him in the right pasture during the day. He's a gelding so don't worry about Coco," Jo explained.

"Sort of sad," Brad said. "I'd like to have a colt conceived on your farm."

Jo laughed at the irony of his statement. "I think that's Ruben's car headed down the road, "Jo said. "Wonder where he's speeding off to?"

"Couldn't guess. He's a quiet man," Brad answered.

Jo smiled as she watched Ruben's car disappear. She turned and told Brad, "But he's a great listener."

On the ride home, Jo scanned her land, taking in all its valleys and flat meadows. Brad was right; it was ridiculous not to have her own horse to ride out on this land. She'd lost touch with the beauty of the farm and the possibilities it presented.

They stopped at the top of the hill that overlooked her farm-house and fenced pastures. They watched in silence, as Rowdy barked at a frog, the mares swished their tails as they grazed, Little Girl and Nanny followed each other finding tall grass, and the stallion, his noise up, was looking toward Coco.

"I think your stallion has taken a liking to Coco," Brad said. He raised his arm and pointed toward the large, weeping willow tree a half mile from the house. That's the only thing that looks out of place. Who planted that tree?"

"My mom and me, when she was sick with cancer. She told me that whenever I felt alone or lost, I should go there and think about her. My dad called it *my special place.* Told me everyone needs *a special place* all their own." Jo felt Brad's body tighten up as if he'd been hit. She waited, immediately regretting her remark.

"Let's go check it out," Brad said. "Giddy up Coco." They started down the hill toward the large willow.

Brad climbed from the saddle and lifted Jo down until her feet hit the ground. "There's a stream over there," she said pulling him toward it. "I'd skinny dip here all the time. There's a deep part where the water cascades down the hill during rainstorms. Look it rained last night, so it's filled up." She turned and lifted her blouse over her head, her full breasts exposed to his view.

"Am I invited to your special place?" Brad asked, already unbuttoning his shirt.

"You'll be the first man allowed," she announced. Jo sat on the soft, green grass, pulling her boots off. Brad followed her lead. Once naked, they held hands and walked on the slippery mud toward the deep end.

The stream fed the water and it felt cold, yet refreshing. Brad was the first to reach the deep end, testing it to make sure it was safe for Jo. "It's only about three feet deep," and then he sat laughing like a kid. "Come over woman, I want to hold your body."

Jo moved carefully through the mud until she reached him. She placed her arms around his neck and settled down on top of him. He cradled her, his hands roaming over her breasts, his mouth kissing her neck. This is heaven," Brad whispered. "Do you think your mom would approve?"

"Of course; she'd like you very much," Jo answered as she gently turned, using the water to glide her into the perfect position. She placed one leg on either side of him, her face a few inches from his. Jo carefully lowered herself down upon him and back up again; after several excellent repetitions, they both let out a cry of ecstasy.

The sun settled as they lay under the willow branches. "I once had a place of my own," Brad said wistfully. "My dad and I built a tree house in a big tree on our farm. It was the summer before second grade. I spent most of that summer up in that tree." Brad rolled over and using his hands as a pillow, he looked up into the blue sky and continued, "It was my only summer in that tree house. My parents were killed in a car crash that October. Mom was expecting my brother, and he was late coming. I know it was a boy, because I still have the copy of the sonogram. All three were killed."

"I'm so sorry," Jo said. "You were so young. What happened to your farm?"

"The farm was sold; it wasn't as big as yours, only thirteen acres. Dad worked for the post office and farmed when he was home. We loved it. Mom raised chickens and sold their eggs. I hated those chickens and all those eggs. I was the one who had to gather them. The rooster always chased me squawking. I'm glad you don't have any chickens," Brad said laughing.

"Where did you go?" Jo asked gently. "You must've been around seven."

"I went to live with my uncle. He's a good guy and so are his sons. I haven't felt like I had a place all my own since that tree house, though."

Jo raised herself up on her elbow and looked down at him. "You're welcome to share mine. You know that, don't you? It could be home to you, too," she whispered.

Brad sat up admitting, "I only wish that was possible." He stood up and extended his arm toward Jo. "Let's go eat that pot roast. How come every time we eat your pot roasts it's left sitting for hours waiting for us?"

"It's the water. We always have so much fun in water," she said, as she pulled her clothes back on.

The farm was a flurry of activity over the next few days as trucks delivered the extra feed and racing silks.

"Federal Express rocks," Jo said, as she opened the box. "I have to try them on; don't look yet." She ran into the bedroom, leaving

Brad sitting down after a meatloaf dinner, his feet outstretched on her coffee table.

The bedroom door opened and Jo stepped out, her face glowing with pride, her pink and white racing silks fitting perfectly. Brad was not prepared for his own reaction. The sight of her clad in the outfit made the reality of the race frightening. Jo and Little Girl were going to race against all the other men and their huge stallions and mares. His eyes opened wide and he felt physically sick. "Jo, I don't want you to race," he heard himself say.

Jo stared at him, dumbfounded. "Why not?"

"Because I can't protect you out there. I can't help you if you get in trouble," he said, walking over to her. His hands reached down to hold onto her shoulders. He watched the smile cross her lips.

"Brad, you know how stubborn I am. Nothing is going to hurt me. Little Girl and I are going to win that race."

Brad stared into her big, brown eyes and shook his head. "I do love you so much."

"I know," Jo whispered, as she felt him lift her in his arms and take her into the bedroom.

When the truck arrived with the new racing cart, Ruben's face turned pale. Jo looked over at him as they all circled the cart making sure everything was as specified. Ruben walked away into the barn, shaking his head. Jo signed for the cart and followed him, welcoming the cool of the stone building.

Ruben stood in front of Hero's empty stall. Jo walked to his side and then moved in front of Ruben to ask, "Will you come to the race? Please Ruben, I want you there." She saw his eyes move away from hers, his shoulders lift up and then back down again.

"I was there last time," he said, unable to make eye contact.

"This time it will be different. I've grown up; I'm a wiser driver," she said, raising her hand to his arm.

"I don't think I can make it," Ruben said shaking his head '*No*'.

Jo stood on her tiptoes and put her arms around his neck. She whispered into his ear, "You have to make it, Grandpa. You have to tell my child all about the race when the youngster gets old enough. After all, there are two of us racing. It's kiddo's race, too." She settled back onto her flat feet and saw the tears in his eyes. She just winked.

"I'll be there, Jo," Ruben said. "I might bring Audrey." He smiled and shrugged.

"What was that all about?" Brad asked as Jo walked back outside.

Ruben was hesitating about coming to see the race," she said smiling. "I told him no excuses were allowed." She turned and looked over at Brad, "You'll be there, won't you?"

"Nothing, absolutely nothing will keep me away. I might even bunk in with you the night before. I'd feel better if I could," he added.

"Why?" Jo asked. "Are you afraid I can't take care of myself?"

"I've served as a groom one year at the fairgrounds in Georgia. Things can get out of hand the night before a race. Crazy things can happen," Brad explained.

"I know what you mean," Jo agreed. "Some men drink, some gamble, some play guitar, some don't talk at all. It can get weird the night before the race. Come bunk with me, but no romance," she warned.

"No, I'll just be there as a bodyguard," Brad suggested.

"No. You'll be there as part owner," Jo said.

Fifteen

"How'd you like to take a ride with me to York on Saturday?" Jo asked, as she handed Brad the bowl of chili.

"That's a great idea. I've been wanting to see the track," Brad said smiling.

"First we need to see the bondsman and sign the papers making you part owner of Little Girl," Jo informed him, "then we can file the paperwork with the race committee."

"I didn't expect you to make me part owner. You can pay me back some other way," Brad said, with a smirk.

"You staked our race; you deserve to share in the profits," Jo said emphatically.

"Jo, that's a serious thing. Little Girl might have a very, good future ahead of her. We better be on the same page before you make me part owner," Brad warned.

"What do you mean?"

"If I'm part owner, that means I have a say in what happens in her future, like whether she continues racing or returns to the farm to be bred," Brad said.

"What's your philosophy on that?" Jo asked, as she began pouring him a glass of wine.

"I'd like to hear your dream scenario first," Brad said. "What if Little Girl does well at the track, proves she's one of those horses that loves to race? What do you plan to do? Are you willing to drive her in all the races that follow?"

"Not me," Jo answered, watching his expression relax into a smile. "This will be the last race I drive."

"I'm surprised," Brad admitted. "I thought you were in this for the thrill of the race. I've seen trainers that can't give up racing their horses. They end up more driver than trainer, but they don't care. Racing is glamorous, thrilling and the fame can be infectious."

"I've had fame," Jo explained. "I'm famous for being the woman who crashed. No, "I'm in it for something very different." She looked up and smiled at Brad.

"I know, to save your farm," Brad said looking down and breaking off a piece of Italian bread.

Jo wanted to tell him that now it was about winning money so he could buy doc's practice and become daddy to their baby. She noticed the irritation around his mouth and chose a different approach. "I'm in it for the thrill of proving the worth of my stallion and myself as a trainer. I want to spend my time here, breeding him, increasing our farm's worth. I want to develop a line of winners, so I can go to the track and watch. Someday," she said with a smile," I might have kids who'll be like me, enjoy being raised on a horse farm." She stopped and looked over at Brad. "That's my dream scenario."

"What if Little Girl doesn't take to another driver? You could be forced to drive her for this season," Brad said.

"No, April is coming," Jo said, a small smile on her lips. "No, Little Girl will have to race with another driver or not at all. I need to be here on the farm protecting my foals."

Brad watched her eyes light up at the mention of April and the new colts. Relief washed over him, and he said, "That's all good, so I'd love to become part owner of Little Girl." They smiled at each other in agreement, and then Brad asked, "She could end up racing for purses over $500,000. Who's going to drive her?"

"We'll have to find someone," Jo admitted. "She'll have Nanny and we'll find a good, reliable driver. I'll be her trainer, go to the races, but I won't drive again."

"I'm relieved," Brad admitted. "I couldn't handle you driving more races. It's so dangerous, Jo. I'd worry about you."

"That's good to hear. See, owning part of Little Girl will keep us connected. You'll have to stay in touch with me. All those pictures of the two of us standing in the winner's circle will be fun."

"Stubborn," Brad said smiling. "You are so stubborn."

"I prefer the word determined," Jo said walking toward Brad. "Very determined," she added as she handed him a glass of wine.

"What about you?" Brad asked. "Aren't you joining me?"

"No, I'm in training. No more wine, just good healthy food. Little Girl's not the only one that's got to get used to that new racing cart. I forgot how much harder they are to drive. I've got to lean way back in the stretches and balance myself carefully," Jo admitted.

"After we get back from York, I'll watch you on the cart. What does Little Girl think of it?" Brad asked.

"I honestly think she doesn't care. All that horse wants to do is go fast. She's improving every day," Jo said laughing.

After the papers were filed, they stood, staring at the racetrack. "Where did you have the accident?" Brad asked, his eyes shielded by his baseball cap.

"At the southwest corner, right after the viewing stand. See that white fence around the drainage ditch; he drove me right into that and I flipped over the fences," Jo explained, shivering as she stared at it.

"That's the only fenced-in area around this track, and that's only four feet long. Sam Randolph planned this," Brad said, turning with fury in his eyes.

"I've heard that from some spectators. They said it was deliberate."

"Why?" Brad asked. "He was putting himself and his own horse at risk."

"I've been told that he'd been drinking, had himself all worked up. He'd heard how fast my stallion was, saw what a strong animal I was driving. He was sure his record was going to fall," Jo said. "No one can prove any of it, though."

"Did you ride the rail?" Brad asked.

"Yes, I always try to. That's how I train my horses," Jo said, curious.

"Let's walk the track; I want to feel the tilt on the corners. Little Girl is used to running on flat ground," Brad urged.

Brad asked permission of a worker in the grandstand to come through and walk on the racetrack. The man recognized Jo, saying, "Aren't you the woman that had that terrible crash a couple of years ago?"

"Yes, I am," Jo admitted.

"That was the worst accident I've ever seen, and I've been here for forty years. When that cart flew up in the air, I thought you were a goner," the man said, shaking his head. "Knew the horse would never run again. He was hurt so bad. It was awful." He shook his head as if still haunted by the accident. He looked at Jo and asked, "You're not gonna drive again, are you?"

"Yes, I am. Make sure you come see me. Little Girl and I are going to win," Jo said, patting him on the arm.

"You got some nerve, lady," he said, while he unlocked the doors. "I don't care what they say; you got the right to walk this track."

Brad and Jo stepped onto the track, the blue chip stones crunching under their boots. Jo walked to the middle and looked around, taking in a deep breath.

Although empty, she envisioned six, sweating horses pounding around the track, the racing carts and drivers whipping their steeds toward the finish line. She closed her eyes, remembering the sound of their chaotic hoofs keeping pace, their hot breath blowing onto her neck from inches behind. Jo reached down and picked up a handful of the gravel, dust fell through her fingers and she remembered the clouds that rose from the track, choking her breath and caking onto her goggles.

"Are you all right?" Brad asked, seeing her reaction.

"I'll be fine, but did you hear that man? That's all they remember about my stallion and me. Now you see why I have to do this?" Jo said turning to stare up into his blue eyes.

"I understand, Jo, but I'm going to do everything I can to make this ride successful and safe for you. Are you open to my suggestions?" he asked.

"Yes, you've as much say as I do in what goes on in this race. We both have a lot riding on the safety of me and our horse," she said, again preparing to tell him about their baby.

"No, we don't. Please Jo, remember that I'm leaving soon. We'll stay in touch because of Little Girl, but this is nothing more than a long goodbye. You know that, don't you?" Brad said, looking away.

Jo felt deflated by his words. She watched as he clenched his teeth, the muscle movement in his jaw giving away his pain. "I'll try to remember," Jo said.

Brad looked down at Jo, his heart aching to take her into his arms. Instead, he walked a few feet away to where the truck would drop the starting gate. "So this is an oval half-mile track. Right here the horses will be running together, behind the truck and the starting gate. Has Little Girl ever run behind a car yet?" Brad asked.

"No, I better start doing that for her. I can have Ruben drive the farm truck," Jo thought making a mental note.

"Did you train the stallion for the gate?" Brad asked.

"No, and it wasn't a problem. All he wanted to do was run. He didn't care about the other horses, the gate, anything. He just wanted to be in front of every one of them," Jo said, smiling sadly.

"That's all good. Maybe Little Girl's the same way. Still, I think we should have her run behind the truck for as long as she will during the race. Then we'll come up with something that sounds like the gates are opening, and you can train her to take off at a good pace," Brad suggested as Jo took notes. "Have her run the entire race on the outside. Don't hug the rail. This way, Sam Randolph won't be able to push you back into the fence. If he plans to run you down, he'd have to move out to get you and everyone in the stands will see it."

"Little Girl will have to cover a longer distance."

"Yes, but she won't have to contend with the other horses boxing her in. The stallion is hands higher than Little Girl; the big horses around him didn't threaten him. She's so little and they'll be much bigger, so she might get overwhelmed. If you run her on the outside, Little Girl won't realize how big they are. She'll have a clear run to the finish line; she'll like that. Besides, she's used to running alone."

"No one would expect me to race my horse on the outside," Jo admitted. "She'll feel the bank of this track and it might scare her, Jo said as she noticed the tilt.

"She'll think it's the new racing bike. I've got a few ideas on how we can get Little Girl ready for this race. We'll have to time exactly how long it will take us to trailer Little Girl to the fairgrounds. How many days are left before the race?" Brad asked.

Jo stared at him in disbelief, "You don't know?"

"I've been avoiding thinking about it," Brad admitted. "I leave right after the race."

Jo closed her eyes and took a deep breath. "One week," she said through gritted teeth. "We have one week left." She raised her head, and he saw the tears running down her cheeks.

"We need to walk the track; I want you to remember every inch of it so you can plan your attack. Sam Randolph got you right after the first trip around the track, right?" he said as they passed the white fencing around the drainage ditch. "Here, let's stop and look it over." Brad suggested. "Sit up on this fence and look around."

"I don't want to," Jo said, staring at the cement ditch where she hit her head and broke her bones. She remembered the cart whirling over her head, the sound of it crashing, pulling her poor stallion back. Then she remembered the sound of her stallion, screaming in agonized pain, his eyes looking around to see her, as if he was more afraid for her than himself. Poor Hero," Jo said covering her face with her hands. "He spared me, did everything he could not to hurt me," she said, leaning against the fence.

"Hero?" Brad said. "Do you realize that was the first time you ever called that horse by his name? You always just call him the stallion."

His name is Hero," Jo said looking up, daring him to question it. "That's just what he was that day. I'd have been killed if Hero hadn't sacrificed himself to keep from falling on top of me."

"This is too much for you," Brad said. "We shouldn't have come here."

"Yes, we should have," Jo said whipping her tears away with the back of her hand. "He was named Hero because he was stronger, faster, and braver than any horse we had ever seen. He was magnificent. Still is. He carries himself proudly, with only a slight limp. I love that horse; he'll always be my hero."

Jo turned and stared at Brad. "He never let me down and I didn't let him down. Sam Randolph went after both of us and he'll pay for that. I don't care what you say; I'm going to break that jackass's record. Little Girl and I are going to do it," Jo said, before she stood up and began walking around the track, her hands held in front as if she were holding reins.

Brad watched Jo, a lump in his throat. She was so small and so was her horse. Yet, she was so damn determined. *I will never find another woman like Jo. She is going to always be the love of my life,"* he thought as he breathed in and sighed. *I can't keep seeing her. I can't do this to me or to her. It's too hard on both of us. It has to end and soon. It has to end tomorrow."* Brad looked up and watched; she had stopped, talking to herself, making notes on the red tablet she always kept in her back pocket. *"She'll be all right. I need one more night with her. At least I can give myself that,"* he decided.

Brad approached Jo, noticing her face was smudged with a dirt streak. She'd unconsciously twisted her hair into two pigtails, keeping it out of her way while she continued to chart each quarter mile of the track.

"I've got it now! I've marked spots to remind me where I'll be, so I'll know how far I've got to go. Last time, there was so much dust, I couldn't get my bearings. This will work for me," she said, looking up and smiling.

"If you're done," Brad said, "let's go pick out the stall where you, Nanny, and Little Girl will spend the night before the race."

"What about you? You're part owner; you should be there too," she said, stopping to pick up a handful of the track coating. She shoved it into a plastic bag she'd pulled out of her other back pocket. Jo noticed Brad watching her with curiosity. "I'm going to let Little Girl smell this. It smells different than her track. I want to give her as much information as possible."

She shoved the dirt filled pack into her pocket and strode toward the stadium doorway. Brad watched as she walked back up to the custodian.

"Thanks. What's your name?" Jo asked.

"I'm Trevor," the man said, taking off his baseball hat.

"Trevor, will you do me a favor?" Jo asked.

"Anything I can. I don't have much I can do though," Trevor admitted.

"Will you tell everyone who's interested, that Hero's daughter, Little Girl, is going to beat the driver who drove him off the track? Remember that the stallion's name was Hero, because that is what he was. He saved my life that day. You were right to think I was a goner. Hero saved me. Now his daughter's going to have revenge."

"I'll tell ''em," Trevor said, licking his lips. "That's right, the horse was called Hero. You got it, lady. Give Sam Randolph hell."

"How do you know his name? Jo asked.

"Because he shows up every year, gets drunk and nasty on the night before the race. He yells at all of us like we're dirt under his feet. Walks around like cock of the barnyard. He's a prick," Trevor said before shoving his hand over his mouth.

"That he is," Jo said laughing. "That he is."

Sixteen

"Where was your stall when Hero raced?" Brad asked, as they strode toward the two long barns. Each barn was painted a soft gold with green and white trim. There was no center walkway, just ten-foot, square stalls built back to back. Individual doors were the only way in or out, the solid wood walls keeping the horses isolated. The stall doors were split in half so when the top half was opened, the horses could look out the door despite being penned in the stall.

"Hero's stall was the farthest one from the midway. It was on the backside of that barn, the quietist one I could find. This place gets crazy once the fair opens," Jo explained, as they headed toward the far building. "The York Fair is the oldest fair in America. Matter of fact, it started in 1765, eleven years before America was founded."

"Really," Brad asked, "and it's still going strong?"

"Wind it up and it goes ten days," Jo said with a laugh, as she walked up to Hero's old stall.

"Wind it up?" Brad asked.

"That's the Fair's slogan. There's a song that accompanies it, but you already know I don't sing."

Brad lost all interest in fair history; he was focused on construction of the individual stalls. "How did Hero handle the new quarters?" Brad asked, as he looked inside and pounded on the thick wooden walls.

"He seemed to enjoy the change," Jo said, watching Brad.

"I'm glad they extended the roof of the barn out five feet. It'll keep the horses dry if it rains. It also gives them shade. Where did you sleep?" Brad asked.

"Most drivers bring their own trailers and bunk down in rows a few feet from the stalls. I slept in the Silverado Inn," she said with a grin.

"Where?" Brad asked, as he continued scrutinizing the area.

"I put the seat down and slept in the back of my old Silverado truck," Jo said grinning.

"Not very private," Brad said, looking over at Jo.

"Harness racers are only here for one or two nights. I've slept in worse places," Jo admitted.

"Really?" Brad asked suddenly intrigued. "Where was the worst place?"

"I once spent the night sleeping on the ground with my purse for a pillow," Jo admitted, as she walked back up the row of stalls toward the end.

"Why?" Brad asked.

"I had one serious relationship in my life. Turns out he thought of it as a fling. Once I figured that out, I told him to pull over and let me out," Jo explained as they turned the corner and walked toward the other row of stalls. "I walked into the Georgia woods."

"What?" Brad said stopping, his hands rising to his hips. "You could have been hurt, snake bit or worse."

"It wasn't his idea to leave me out there; I refused to get back in the car. He said he parked there until morning, but I wouldn't know if that's true or not. My cell phone didn't work out there, so

I slept on a patch of soft grass beside a creek. The frogs sang all night long. In the morning, I had a triumphant six-mile walk back to school. It was freeing," Jo announced.

Brad looked down into her brown eyes. "You are a force to be reckoned with. How long did you go with this man?" Brad asked.

"Six months," Jo stated.

"I can't believe any man could walk away from you after six months," Brad said.

"He didn't," Jo explained. "I broke it off after I realized he wasn't interested in the same things I was. I've always wanted a farm filled with children and horses," Jo explained. "He wanted to be carefree and wild."

"How old were you?" Brad asked.

"I was twenty-one; so was he," Jo admitted. An uneasy quiet filled the space between them. Brad walked over to a bench and sat down. She followed him. Still standing, Jo looked down into his eyes and asked, "While we're on the subject, do you want the same things I do?" Brad's eyes dropped. Jo sat down next to him, holding her breath.

"I'm afraid to tell you what I want. You might not give me a ride back to the farm," Brad said. He raised one hand to comb through his hair, one of the many movements Jo found endearing. She knew he was selecting his words carefully. "Honesty, is that what you want?" Brad finally asked.

"Yes, I think people waste too much time faking things. Be honest with me, please."

"I never want to have kids," Brad said as he reached down and picked up some pebbles. He tossed one toward a fence, as if he was throwing away their future. Jo felt familiar stabs of heartbreak.

"Why?" was all she could utter.

"I've experienced the pain children can bring," Brad said, avoiding her eyes. "My parents didn't plan to have any more children. They were happy with just one kid. We weren't rich, but we had all we needed. Mom worked as the school secretary. She and I had the same holidays, so they didn't need to pay babysitters. We had a good life, but I wanted a big family. Most of my friends lived on farms and they all had sisters and brothers. They were always having adventures together. I wanted what they had," Brad admitted.

"I did too," Jo said, as she forced herself to calm her nerves. "I wanted Mom to have more kids. They tried, but Mom got sick and we all knew it would never happen. That's why I want at least two, maybe four kids."

"Jo," Brad reminded her, "my mom and dad were killed coming home from the doctor's appointment."

Jo's eyes opened wide, as she connected information. "Oh!" she whispered.

Brad threw a pebble and they both watched it bounce off a fence post. "When Mom and Dad told me about the baby coming, I felt like the luckiest kid in the world. As far as I was concerned, I persuaded them to have another kid, so it was my baby, my responsibility." His hand rose again and he threw three more pebbles hitting nothing but empty air. "I remember everything about that time. They let me paint the nursery. I painted it this yellow color with light blue trim. I thought I did a good job, but looking back, I know I wasn't a very neat painter." They both laughed.

"That was nice of them" Jo offered.

"Yeah," they always made me feel special. My dad and I put the crib up together; he let me screw in the bolts. It was the happiest time in my life," Brad admitted. "So many dreams about what I'd do with the kid once it grew up a little."

"So you have happy memories," Jo said, gaining hope.

"If Mom hadn't gotten pregnant, they would still be alive," Brad said letting the remaining pebbles drop to the ground. He dusted off his hands, signaling the end of the discussion.

"You can't blame yourself for the accident," Jo said reaching out to take his hand.

Brad pulled away and stood up. "It might not make sense, but I don't want to ever go through that again."

"Through what?" Jo asked confused.

"I don't think I was meant to have any kids. I'm not interested in a farm full of kids any more. Too many things can go wrong. I'd never sleep at night. I don't want the same things as you, Jo," Brad said shrugging. "Do you hate me?"

"No," Jo said shaking her head. "I feel sorry for you. You're going to miss out on love, joy, and happiness."

Brad looked away toward the next barn. "You're probably right, but it is what it is. You sit tight while I go check out the next row of barns."

Jo sat numb while he took strong strides, as if eager to put distance between them both. I'm a fool, Jo thought, shaking her head. How could I have been so stupid? I just made up some fantasy ending with Brad as an adoring father and husband. He doesn't want any part of that life.

Jo waited until he turned the corner to investigate the stalls on the row facing the fairgrounds. Only then did she slide her hand over to gently rest on her tummy. "We're going to be all right, little one. I love you. You and I are going to win this blasted race, and then we'll be able to raise horses that'll race like the wind. Don't you worry, little one," Jo said standing up, "we'll always have each other."

Jo's eyes squinted toward the metal sculpture being raised in front of the last row of stalls. It stood around a hundred feet from the barn. Brad was signaling her to join him at the end of the row.

"I think this is the stall for you," he said, avoiding eye contact.

"Are you kidding me?" Jo said. "That monstrosity they are building is going to be the loudest ride in the fair. It's a roller coaster. It will be surrounded by a Ferris wheel and heaven knows what else. That is the mechanical ride section of the fair. There will be blinking lights, loud music, teenagers and kids screaming on the rides."

"Can you imagine how interesting that will be to Little Girl and Nanny? They'll love it. It will keep their minds off the boring, wooden box they'll be in. Besides that," Brad said, "when Little Girl enters the racetrack, she won't even notice the sound of the bugle blowing or the announcer. She'll even be used to the crowd shouting. It's perfect!"

Jo shook her head; "She might not get any sleep."

"They have to turn the rides off when the fair closes. Think about it a minute. What did Hero do when you entered the racetrack?" Brad asked.

Jo looked up at Brad, admitting, "I can't remember. I was overwhelmed. Let me think." She looked toward the ramp leading to the track. Suddenly it all came back to her. "We rode up that ramp, and Hero almost stopped. It was as if he wanted to protect me from the other horses and the crowd." She looked over at Brad. "I remember that now. You're right. He wasn't prepared for all the people or strange noises."

"This is your stall," Brad said with a smile. "We'll bring Little Girl and Nanny here early in the morning, They'll have all day to study the fair. By the time of the race, she'll think the track is quiet." They both laughed.

"Are we still friends?" Brad asked as they walked toward the registration office.

'We'll always be friends," Jo admitted. "We co-parent Little Girl."

"Keep track of the time it takes us to get to your farm," Brad suggested. "When we get there, I think we should hitch up the trailer and take Nanny and Little Girl for a ride for that amount of time. The more exposure they have to things that will happen next week, the better they'll handle them."

"That's a good idea," Jo said leaning back. "Remember how hard it was to get poor Nanny out of the truck the first time you brought her to the farm?" They both laughed. "Where did you ever get her from?" Jo inquired.

"I'd been on a call at Mummer's farm the week before. Nanny insisted on sitting next to his barn, bellowing at the horses. It sounded like she was calling Ma, Ma. All the other goats were out in the pasture having a great time chewing on the tall grass around the fence posts."

"See," Jo said, tilting her head. "Some of us need to be mothers."

"And some of us need to be old goats roaming around for food," Brad said.

"And you said you were no old goat," Jo said patting his leg.

"I guess I was wrong," Brad admitted, in a sad, furlong tone.

They tried to put Nanny in the trailer first; she screamed as if being tortured. Her terrorized sounds made Little Girl uneasy and she began neighing, frantically running around the pen.

Brad brought Nanny out and the goat ran to the horse. They both checked each other over.

"Little Girl has to go in first," Brad suggested.

Jo led Little Girl up the ramp, and Nanny began running around the pen bellowing. That made Little Girl rear up and she had to be taken out of the trailer.

"Both have to get on at the same time, but they won't fit on the ramp," Brad complained.

"Open the gate so Nanny can get out," Jo suggested. She led Little Girl up the ramp, Nanny trotting directly behind them. Jo secured them and closed up the trailer. They listened for sound of protest, but none came.

"Let's see what happens when the truck starts," Brad suggested. He climbed in and started the engine. No movements or sounds erupted. "We're good to go," he called out to Jo. "Jump in."

They eased out of the driveway, timing their ride. "Any other ideas?" Jo asked once they were on a smooth road.

"Yes, I've got a lot of them. Do you think Ruben will come over tomorrow?" Brad asked.

"It's his day off, but he will if I need him," Jo explained.

"We do. I'd like him to drive your truck around the track, as if he was the starting truck. I think I need to bring Coco into the track and keep her on the inside rail while you train Little Girl to ride on the outside. I want to see how Little Girl handles running against another horse," Brad explained.

"You think your quarter horse can keep up with my pacer?" Jo said with a smirk.

"Quarter horses are the fastest horses around for the first quarter mile. That's why they're called quarter horses," Brad answered.

"Wanna bet?" Jo challenged.

"Absolutely," Brad said. "What are we betting?"

"If my horse wins, you have to muck out the farm stall during our stay at the track," Jo suggested.

"It's our horse, so I can't lose," Brad announced. "Besides, I planned to do that anyway."

"I can't win," Jo said shrugging. Their eyes met and Brad shrugged.

"Can you think of someone else to come help out on Sunday?" he asked changing the subject. "I'd like to film this fiasco, so we can take a look at what we can do to help Little Girl."

"Yes, I know just the person. I'll call Ruben and he can invite her," Jo said reaching for her phone.

At the end of the drive, Nanny and Little Girl trotted off the truck as if they did it every day. Jo led them out to their pasture while Brad unhitched the trailer. He watched as the three crossed the pasture. *They belong to each other. They belong here on this farm,*" he thought wistfully. *I wonder if I'll ever find where I belong?* Just then, his cell phone rang. Brad reached for it, his eyes not leaving Jo. "Hello," he said flatly.

"Brad, I've got great news," his uncle's voice said into the phone. "I got a call from a friend of mine in Australia. One of the big horse farms is looking for a vet. It's a permanent position. I sent them the resume you left and they just emailed me that they want you. They're willing to hire you for a year minimum with the hope of keeping you on permanently. They'll pay all your expenses," his uncle announced.

"Really?" Brad said as he watched Jo take her usual seat on the fence post. She was looking over her farm, making sure everything was as it should be.

"Send me the email," Brad suggested. "I'll check it out and get back to them. When do they need an answer?"

"They want you ASAP," his uncle announced. "I'll send it to you. Great news; I'm happy for you."

"It is great news," Brad said, as he took in a deep sigh. "Thanks for your help. I'll always be in your debt for all you've done for me."

"You did it all yourself," his uncle announced. "Your mom and dad would've been so proud."

"Can I ask you something?" Brad inquired, surprising himself.

"Anything," his uncle stated.

"Did Mom or Dad ever talk to you about the baby?" Brad asked.

"What?" his uncle asked.

"I know it's a senseless question, but I always wondered if they ever said anything to you about the baby on the way," Brad said.

"Yes, of course they did. Your dad told me that he always had envied my crew of sons. Said he couldn't believe he was lucky enough to have another kid," his uncle explained, "but your mother was a whole different story. She couldn't stop talking about the baby. Said she didn't know who was more excited about the new one, you or her."

"Thanks," Brad said, as tears ran down his face. "You have no idea how much that means to me." Brad cut the connection and looked around the farm. He imagined it with little kids running around. *Did she say she wanted four?* Brad thought. *What a dream that would be. I'd be the luckiest man in the world. Fate seems to have other plans, but Australia? Could I get any farther away? Maybe that would be a good thing. If I lived closer, I'd be here every weekend.*

Seventeen

No words were needed. They both knew that this was the last time they would be intimate. Their agreement to be friends with benefits would end in the morning, and their long goodbye would end with the race.

It seemed fitting that he would grill steaks while she played the guitar. She sat on the wall, barefoot, in just a tee shirt and clean jeans. She smelled like soap and water, and neither had suggested bathing together or in the pond. The impulsive pattern of their former behavior had ended, now every move would be intentional so that the memories would be potent and meaningful.

They moved as though they were in slow motion, breathing in each sensation. The warm breeze that tantalized their skin, the sweet aroma of the blooming mums, the sizzle of the steak, the soft notes gently strum by her fingers all provided a highly sensual preamble to the end of their love story.

"I'm glad we had this time together," Jo said over the flicker of the candle. She watched him sip from his wineglass, his eyes looking down watching her painted fingernails gently tap the black, metal candlestick. She stopped the movement, knowing it showed her uneasiness.

"What will you remember the most?" Brad said lifting his blue eyes to meet her warm, brown orbs.

"It's been such a rush of emotions," Jo admitted, smiling. "I can't remember how I was before you came into my life. I think I was cold and boring. Every day was more about surviving and not much about enjoying life. You taught me what fun life can be. Thank you for that," she said lifting her lemonade glass and taking a long drink.

"What about you?" she said as she looked down and cut her steak.

"I've never allowed myself to get so close to anyone," Brad admitted. "You talk about having one other relationship. Truth is, I haven't had one before you. I'm not saying that I didn't enjoy the companionship of women, but I realize I always chose women who were completely wrong for me. Isn't that strange?"

"What do you mean?" Jo asked as she buttered her potato.

"High maintenance, fancy women," Brad said as though disgusted. "Ones that would never jump in a pond or walk barefoot in mud."

"Really?" Jo said laughing. "I can't see you with those women."

"I think that's why I dated that type. I knew they'd never become anything serious," Brad said.

"You didn't want to have a serious relationship?" Jo asked.

"I guess I didn't," Brad admitted. "I think I was protecting myself from losing someone I cared about again."

"Sounds like you need therapy," Jo admitted. "I strongly suggest my therapist; his name is Ruben."

"Ruben?" Brad asked laughing. "I can't imagine him speaking more than a few words."

"He doesn't," Jo admitted. "You have to listen when he does. When he says something, you can take it to the bank."

"Still can't imagine it," Brad said before biting into his steak.

"I was blaming myself for my dad's death," Jo said. "A person can really do a job on themselves if someone doesn't wise them up."

"I know how that goes," Brad admitted.

"Ruben heard me crying, saw me losing my temper over everything. He knew what was going on. Finally he stopped by the house one day and knocked on the door. I answered, still in my bathrobe holding a box of tissues. He looked at me and said, "You need to talk to your father.""

"I said, he's dead, remember?" Jo admitted, shaking her head. Ruben looked me in the eyes and said, "You now have two fathers in heaven. Talk to them." Then he turned and walked down the steps and drove away."

"Wow," Brad said, putting his fork down.

"Now I talk to both my dad and the heavenly father every night, usually there on the porch swing, where my dad and I would rock each night. Now I understand what my dad would tell me, if he were still alive," Jo admitted. "It makes everything easier. I never feel alone."

"I'll have to try that," Brad said. "I've always pushed down all memories of my parents. Maybe I'll have to try that." They both smiled at each other. "We are alike in so many ways," Brad admitted.

"That we are," Jo said, "but it's the differences I like the most."

"Differences?" Brad asked intrigued. "How are we different?"

"You don't walk, you sort of stomp. I love to hear you walk through the house," Jo said laughing.

"You always walk on your tiptoes once those boots are off," Brad said. "Did you know that? Like you were toe dancing."

"I do not?" Jo asked. She thought awhile, "Maybe I do. I've always worn the highest heels I could find; even my work boots have big heels. I'm sick of being so short."

"I like you just the way you are," Brad said. "Small but mighty."

"I do have impressive muscles," Jo said, lifting her arms and flexing one bicep.

"See what I mean?" Brad said laughing. "What other woman would flash me her bicep." They both laughed.

"I like how you bellow around the farm. Ruben and I are both so quiet," Jo said, eating some of her potato.

"I'll miss the soft sounds you make when you're sleeping. Sometimes I lay awake for hours just so I won't miss hearing them," Brad admitted.

"What sounds," Jo asked amazed.

"Soft, puffing sounds, and sometimes you talk in your sleep," Brad explained.

"I do not," Jo said, suddenly concerned. "What do I say?"

"Nothing interesting; I just think it's cute," Brad said. "Last night you said go to sleep little one."

Jo's hand rose to her face, "I did?"

"Yes, I could take that as an insult you know," Brad said raising his eyebrows.

"Like I would call anything on your body, little one," Jo said blushing. "I was just thinking about the fouls coming in April. I love fouling season."

"I don't," Brad admitted. "I love to help bring life into the world, but I've had so many heartbreaking births. I get called out when a horse gets in trouble, remember?" Brad said.

"I forgot that," Jo admitted.

"I've had to do some terrible things to save a horse or its colt," Brad said.

"Don't tell me. I've heard about some horrific stories in college. I can't imagine," Jo admitted.

"Maybe that's why I consider birth so dangerous," Brad explained.

"Are you doing the dishes or am I?" Jo said changing the subject.

"Let's do them together," Brad suggested.

They worked together, only the soft sound of the horses neighing in the field broke the silence. "I'm feeling nervous," Jo admitted, as she washed the last dish.

"So am I," Brad agreed. "I can't imagine that this is the last time we'll make love. I want to make everything perfect."

"Perfect is boring," Jo said smiling. "You've never been boring in your life. Maybe we should do the opposite of perfect."

"What are you suggesting?" Brad asked.

"Let's make love where we've never made love before," Jo suggested.

"Like the barn? We've never made love in the barn," Brad said, grabbing her hand and tossing her over his shoulder.

They entered the barn and Brad carried her to the last stall. It was Coco's stall, and it was filled with a clean layer of straw. Coco was out in the pasture. Brad laid Jo down very gently, grateful that the full moon shone through the barn window.

Jo smiled up at him and slowly slipped off her tee shirt. Brad removed his shirt and unbuckled his belt. His jeans fell from his waist, and he kicked off all clothing as she squirmed out from her jeans. He stood above her, studying her body lying on the straw before him. She did the same, memorizing every inch of his legs, stomach, arms and of course his testament of desire. Brad lowered himself onto Jo and there, draped in moonlight, they joined in slow, pulsating movements.

They lay beside each other tracing each other's bodies with fingertips and kisses until they fell asleep.

Jo nudged Brad and he awoke startled. "In the meadow," Jo whispered, and she bent down to kiss and arouse him again. She stood up and ran out of the stall toward the meadow, Brad in hot pursuit.

The grass in the meadow was damp with dew and soft in comparison to the hay. Jo rolled around and around in the damp grass and Brad joined her. "I'm cold now," she laughed as she stood up above him.

"Come here; I'll warm you up," he said extending his arms.

"She laid on top of him, rubbing in long, slow movements. His hands rose to her back and stopped her. "Hold still woman," he demanded, and his mouth found one nipple. In the meadow, they tasted, kissed and experienced each other while Rowdy stood guard on top of the hill. His breathing and grunts accentuated their own. It was perfect.

"I can't fall asleep here but I'm exhausted," Brad admitted.

"Let's go back to our bed," Jo said, before realizing what she said.

"I wish it would always be our bed," Brad said when he saw the sadness in her eyes.

"You know I want that too," Jo said gently. "More than you know."

"We should rest," Brad said as they held hands and walked toward the farmhouse. "Right after we make love in the Silverado Inn."

The sun woke them in time to gather their clothes and move discreetly into the bedroom. The soft sheets felt wonderful after the smorgasbord of textures experienced throughout the night. "This is the most comfortable bed in the world," Brad announced as he slid under the sheets. "I'm too exhausted to make good use of it," he admitted.

"Shush," Jo suggested. "I need sleep."

They were still sleeping, wrapped in each others arms when they heard Ruben's car pull down to the barn. They both opened their eyes and stared at each other. A tear slipped down Jo's cheek.

"Life isn't fair," she whispered.

"No, it isn't," Brad said as he slipped out of bed. "I will always love you," he said as he pulled on his clothes. He stopped and looked down at her, "Always and forever. No matter how far I go."

Eighteen

"Hi Ruben," Brad said as he walked into the barn. "We really appreciate you coming over on your day off." Ruben nodded and leaned against the wall, saying nothing. "Have you had coffee yet?" Brad asked.

"Yup," Ruben answered, his eyes focused on the driveway.

"Is someone else coming?" Brad prompted.

"Yup," Ruben answered.

"Why don't we wait on the front porch?" Brad suggested, struggling to keep the one-sided conversation going.

Ruben turned and took the long path toward the farmhouse, indicating he wanted to make the trip alone. His demeanor spoke louder than words; Ruben wasn't happy. Brad stood confused watching him walk away, until Ruben stopped, turned and briefly glared at Brad. Then he turned and started up the hill again, kicking a stone as if he were mad at it. Ruben's disapproval stirred up feelings of shame and self-recrimination.

Brad turned away and headed for the privacy of the barn. He sank onto a pile of hay bales that he hadn't gotten around to properly stack. Brad took an appraisal of his behavior, and it left him feeling physically ill.

He hadn't helped with much of the heavy work, too eager to spend time with Jo. He stood and walked out the barn's back door, squinting toward the meadow where Jo had been struggling to put up fencing. He hadn't gotten around to completing the fencing.

On his way back through the barn, he glanced into Coco's stall. Jo's tee shirt still lay on the straw. Brad reached out and picked it up, lifting it immediately to his nose to garner more of her essence. The instinct shocked him and he realized *I've been acting like a 'dog in heat'. Ruben must be disgusted with me. I should have been working, not playing around like a teenager.* Brad walked up to the house anxious to admit to his failings and commit to remedy his mistakes.

Ruben was standing on the front porch. "I need to apologize to you, Ruben," Brad admitted. "I haven't been helping with the heavy work around here."

"No need," Ruben said, as he looked out over the farm.

Brad continued, "I'm moving back to my place tonight. Jo needs to focus on the race. I'll be here whenever I can. I want to hang the fence around the far pasture so it's ready for the foals in April."

"Good. Jo shouldn't be doing heavy work," Ruben said and he turned to look at Brad. The two men stared at each other, Brad waiting for clarification. Instead, Ruben reached over and gently patted Brad's back twice, as if to comfort him. Then Ruben walked into the kitchen, following the smell of coffee brewing.

Brad stood there, trying to figure out what had just happened. He felt that Ruben had told him something important, but he couldn't figure out what. Just then, a car pulled into the driveway, breaking his train of thought.

Brad watched as a grey Toyota Maxima pulled to a stop in front of the house. A smiling woman in her sixties drove it. She sat there watching Brad walk down the steps. He opened the door and extended his hand ready to assist the woman out of the car.

"You must be Brad," Audrey said accepting his assistance. "I'm Audrey Van Order. Jo's mother was my best friend. I now consider myself Jo's mother," Audrey narrated. "I could use your help. I've cooked us all breakfast, lunch and dinner. Will you be a dear and help me bring it inside?"

Brad's eyes opened wide. "I'd be happy to," Brad admitted. As he lifted the carefully packed boxes filled with plastic containers and a pie, he smiled. It reminded him of helping his grandma unload her contributions when she came to his mom and dad's farm on Thanksgiving. This woman's tone had the same melodic quality and pattern as his grandma's voice. Brad was drawn to her.

"Thank you, dear," Audrey said. "You're so kind. Is it too heavy?"

Brad smiled, enjoying both the company and attention of Audrey. "Not at all," he said. "Be careful on the steps." He felt transported to another time, when his family gathered together. He couldn't stop beaming, even when he entered the house.

Brad watched the short woman walk toward Ruben saying, "Hello, dear. Did you eat breakfast?" She stood up on her tiptoe and kissed him lightly on the lips. Brad froze, totally stunned by the act.

"Jo," Audrey then said, as she placed her things on the table. "Let me look at you." The woman moved toward Jo, taking her into her arms and holding her in a warm embrace. They were both the same height and it fascinated Brad. "How are you feeling?" Brad heard her ask.

"Wonderful," Jo said, as she blushed. "I'm not nervous at all about the race. Brad's been helping me get ready." Brad noticed that Jo's eyes flickered over toward him as if to check his reaction.

"Sit and eat something," Audrey demanded. "I brought over an egg casserole. Don't worry, it's very light and won't be too heavy on your stomach."

Jo smiled and sat down, while Audrey fetched plates for everyone. "We all need to build our strength. I have no idea what you two have in mind for us today," Audrey explained. Everyone sat and Brad smiled over at Jo. It was nice to feel like a member of an extended family. He forgot how much he'd missed feeling connected.

"Now don't let me hold up this day," Audrey insisted. "I'll serve and you go ahead and eat while it's still warm. I've already had my fill. Brad, open that green Tupperware dish, will you? It has fruit salad. I'll get you all bowls."

Ruben, Jo and Brad smiled over at each other. Audrey's presence made them all relax. "What are we doing?" Ruben asked as Audrey served him first. Brad watched as her hand caressed his bald head.

Brad waited for Jo to explain, but she looked over at him, putting him in charge. That small transfer of authority validated his place in this strange concoction of people. He was no longer the odd man out. He felt he belonged.

"Jo and I spent several hours at the fairgrounds yesterday. We identified things we need to do to prepare Little Girl for the race. Jo, do you have your notes?" Brad asked.

Jo reached into her back pocket and flipped her notebook to the last few pages. Then she handed Brad her notes. The movement continued to surprise him. He smiled and looked down at the paper. He noticed how neat her writing was, with lots of swirls and circles instead of just periods. Having lived in a world of men, he found it endearing. It touched him, and the tilt of his head and his smile revealed his reaction to everyone around the table.

Brad cleared his throat and began, "Jo and I walked the race-track. We saw the spot of the accident and realized that Sam had planned just where he was going to drive Jo off into the fence."

Ruben pounded his fist onto the table, making all the plates jump. "That bastard," Ruben yelled, surprising everyone.

Audrey reached over and rubbed Ruben's shoulder saying, "There, there, dear."

"We need to train Little Girl to run on the outside, so Sam won't be able to repeat his attack. She'll be safe out there," Brad explained.

"Good idea," Ruben said, pointing his finger at Brad.

"How can we help?" Audrey asked.

"We need to get Little Girl used to being on the track at the same time as the tractor and the starter truck. That's not all," Brad said feeling more confident in his new position of leadership. We need to expose Little Girl to running on the track with other horses."

"I like that!" Ruben said, smiling over at Brad. "How?"

Brad carefully explained his plan for the day, assigning various duties to members around the table. "I haven't the slightest idea how to take videos," Audrey admitted. "Ruben can you show me?"

"I can't help you, honey. Brad, you show her. I'll help Jo clean up the dishes," Ruben said, in the longest sentence anyone had ever heard uttered by the man. Jo and Brad smiled at each other.

The plan unfolded with Ruben pulling the drag behind the tractor. Jo took in a deep breath, flipped her reins and urged Little Girl onto the track, while the tractor continued its work. Little Girl stepped out unimpressed, her legs moving without hesitation. They circled twice while Ruben stayed close to the rail, forcing the horse to the outer ring of the track. Ruben then drove out and the second phase began.

Brad rode Coco onto the track urging the mare to trot between the rail and Little Girl. Jo stiffened on the racing bike, preparing for Little Girl to falter. Instead, her horse increased the pace. Jo held her back, keeping them side by side. They were all warming up for the final phase.

On the second time around for both horses, Ruben pulled the Silverado onto the track. The truck's cap had been removed. In its place, the open bay held two long screen doors tied sideways, both removed from Jo's house. They looked surprising like the metal gates Little Girl would run behind in the race.

Jo slowed Little Girl down and turned her the racing way. Brad did the same with Coco. Now they lined up behind the truck easing their horses into a safe pace behind the moving truck. Little Girl hesitated until she saw the big horse next to her move up and then she lost all fear. They circled the track, keeping at a steady pace. In the real race, this is where the announcer would introduce each horse, the owners and the driver to the crowd in the stands.

The truck continued around the track picking up speed, mimicking what would happen in the official race. Little Girl sped up behind the truck, keeping pace with the quarter horse beside her. Once in front of Audrey and her camera, Ruben gassed the truck, pulling out of the track. The race had started.

Brad kicked Coco and the big horse sprinted, leaving Little Girl in the dust. Jo flicked her reins and Little Girl lunged forward, seemingly desperate to keep up with the other horse. Coco took long, steady strides, while Little Girls legs pounded behind in perfect pacing form, almost catching the big horse in front.

The second quarter, Little Girl began making up ground, closing in on the big, brown horse. Jo let her run at her own pace and Little Girl turned up the speed, her eyes wide with anticipation and determination. By the half-mile, Little Girl and Coco were side by side. Audrey began screaming, as instructed, but neither horse was distracted.

The last mile revealed Little Girl's will. She passed the big horse but never slowed down. Her speed only increased, as if wanting to leave Coco further behind. By the end of the two-mile race, Little Girl had gained three quarters of a mile on Coco.

The camera caught the look of joy on all the faces of the humans working with the horses. The footage would be enjoyed many times over.

Once all the animals had been cooled down, washed and put out to pasture, the humans returned to the house. Audrey opened another of the plastic bowls to uncover her homemade potato salad and fried chicken. They ate around the table watching the film play out on the screen set up in the living room.

Jo watched and felt all her fears slip away. Little Girl was born to race. She would secure the stallion and all his foals' worth. Little Girl could win.

The afternoon found them repeating the same scenario, only Little Girl anticipated what was next. In these films, they could see the horse getting excited, her nostrils flaring at the sight of the truck and the gates. This horse wanted to race.

By the time Audrey served them a spaghetti dinner, they were ready to celebrate. Brad and Ruben drank beer, Audrey and Jo ice tea. It seemed as if they had all shared years of evenings like this. This group's common goal united them closer than one with ancestral pedigree.

"Brad, hasn't this been a wonderful day," Audrey asked. "I'm so glad to finally meet you."

"I'm glad to meet you. You're a great cook, but most of all you make Ruben smile," Brad kidded.

The group all laughed, Ruben slapping his own leg in agreement. "It's getting late, old girl," Ruben said standing. "You have to work tomorrow."

"Where do you work?" Brad asked, as he helped Jo pack up the empty bowls.

"I own the dress store in town—the one where Jo bought that turquoise gown," Audrey said smiling.

"That was the most beautiful gown I'd ever seen," Brad said remembering that night. He flinched when he recalled the image of Jo crumbled into a pool of turquoise crying in the driveway as he pulled out. Tears formed in his eyes and he looked away.

"Walk me out, old man," Audrey said sweetly. Ruben lifted her box of bowls and escorted her to the car.

"How long have they been together?" Brad asked.

"A few weeks," Jo announced.

"That can't be. They seem like they've been in love forever," Brad said turning to look out the door.

"They have been. It's a long, sad story," Jo said dropping her head and looking away.

Brad was disturbed by her answer, but sensed it was time for him to leave as well. He went into the bedroom to gather his things.

Outside, Audrey leaned up and kissed Ruben gently. Then she took hold of both his arms. "Do something about this mess," she demanded.

"It's not my place," Ruben said shaking his head.

"Do it for Jo, for our grandbaby, for us," Audrey urged. "Don't let them waste all the years we lost."

Ruben smiled and whispered, "I'll think of something."

When Ruben returned to the house, he saw Brad had packed and was ready to leave. He also saw Jo's little red notepad on the counter. Ruben picked it up as he walked Brad out to his truck.

"You remind me of myself years ago," Ruben said, shaking his head. "Takes a fool to know a fool." He lifted his hand and handed Brad the notebook.

"That's Jo's," Brad said.

"You better read through it," Ruben said before he tipped his hat and walked toward the barn.

Nineteen

It was 9:30 when Brad climbed the thin, linoleum steps above the twirling studio. He hated those steps; his feet were too big to fit. He hated the way the staircase smelled, like old sneakers and mold. He hated the song they were blaring downstairs, 'Won't You Come Home, Bill Bailey." Brad opened the door to his two rented rooms and looked around at the dingy flat. He looked at the clock; they'd be gone in half an hour, and then he'd have quiet. He shook his head; he didn't want quiet. He wanted to go back to the only place he felt at home. He wanted to crawl into the big, soft bed at Jo's farm and take her in his arms. He wanted to smell her hair and listen to her soft, sleeping sounds.

Brad sat down at his computer and signed on to his email account. Twenty-two messages awaited his attention. He put one foot behind the other and flipped off one boot. Wiggling his toes, he then flipped off the second. It all seemed wrong, sitting on a metal chair in front of a metal, card table with only his computer for company. Brad scrolled down the mail, prioritizing the vet calls. He'd been in Hanover long enough to recognize the names, picture their farms, remember the barns and sometimes even the horse with the problem. He shook his head, realizing that he'd miss being part of their lives.

His fingers hesitated when he saw his uncle's email address. He clicked on the email and read the message, a sick feeling growing in his gut. They wanted him and were prepared to pay him well. It was an Australian thoroughbred horse farm, 2500 acres of prime, fertile land, with manicured grounds, a horse track, and all the medical equipment he could imagine. He'd complete a team of five vets who lived and worked on the horse farm. That's as far as he got. Brad shut down the computer and stomped over to the lumpy mattress that had come with the other lumpy furniture in the cheap, two-room flat. He lay down and listened, as the kids downstairs said giggling good-byes.

"Kids," Brad said shaking his head. "Kids have it made." He smiled when he thought how much Jo wanted kids. "She'd probably stay and watch the dumb practice. She'd love it as much as the kids," he thought, a sentimental smile on his face. He missed her, felt lost without her. Brad had enjoyed the day at the farm and everything about it. He felt needed and part of something. Ruben and Audrey felt familiar to him like he'd known them forever. He wondered why. He knew Audrey reminded him of his maternal grandma. She'd been his favorite relative. She'd died three years after his mom. Ruben didn't remind him of anyone. He was a true character and he fascinated Brad. He was like a puzzle and he kept trying to figure him out. Jo was right. He didn't say much, but he chose his words carefully. Two of Ruben's sentences were more provocative than hours of philosophy lectures, but the day had slipped by too fast, and Brad had the sinking feeling that Ruben had been trying to tell him something.

When Brad heard the owner set the studio alarm and close the door, he realized just how tired he was. He smiled as he remembered why. His eyes closed as he recalled their night of passion, his arms around the pillow as he fell asleep. It was four a.m. when he hit the floor with a thump. His pride was hurt more than his body, and he looked around dazed. The lights were still on; so were his clothes. He checked the clock thinking *I can still get a few hours more sleep*. He was eager to go back to his dreams of Jo, but he stopped in the bathroom first. He was washing his hands when he spotted the little, red notepad stuck in his shirt pocket. It made him smile. He unbuttoned his shirt, carefully putting the notepad on the glass shelf over the sink. He stripped off his clothes and still felt sweaty.

Brad turned on the water in the metal shower stall and stepped in. The water felt good on his body, refreshing despite the cramped, creaky stall. He soaped up, deciding it would give him more time in the morning. When he stepped out and grabbed for a towel, it knocked the red notebook to the floor. He dried his face and body, then picked it up, carrying it with him back to the bed. Brad lay down throwing the towel on the floor. He lifted the notebook to his nose, and he smelled Jo's perfume. *What is that smell?* he pondered. *Honeysuckle*, he realized, proud of himself. The shower had lifted his mood, woken him up. *Ruben said to read this*, Brad recalled. He sat up, remembering the look on Ruben's face when he said it. Brad turned to the pages Jo had written at the track. He reread the lists. *What was he telling me? What did I miss?* Brad thought. Brad stood up and walked to the hotplate; he needed coffee. More of Ruben's cryptic words began bothering him. He'd said something on the porch, just before Audrey arrived. *It wasn't what he said, but the look he'd given me when he said it. The look said 'wake up dummy.' What did he say?* Brad wondered, leaning on the counter watching the coffeepot perk. *It was about the fencing. I promised to fence in the new pasture. Ruben said, 'Jo shouldn't be doing heavy work'.* Brad took down a cup and put it on the counter. He walked over to the window, still waiting for coffee. He parted the stained, canvas drapes and looked out the window. It was dark, just streetlights illuminating the street. A grey car drove slowly past them, sparking another thought, Audrey has a grey car. She said something strange, too. He shuddered as he remembered. *Audrey was holding Jo and asked, "How are you?" Jo's sick. That's why they watch her so closely,* Brad thought. He closed his eyes, trying to remember everything that had happened.

Audrey ran over to Jo after each practice section. Ruben had taken Little Girl and helped Jo out of the cart. He never used to help her out of the cart. Brad had wanted to congratulate Jo and hug her, but Audrey had escorted Jo out the barn door and out of sight. Brad had resigned himself to cooling down Coco. When he'd walked the mare out into her pasture, he'd noticed Audrey and Jo behind the barn. Audrey had told Jo something funny, and Jo was leaned over, hands on her knees laughing. He'd thought it was cute to see them together. He stopped breathing, his eyes growing wide. *No, she wasn't laughing. Audrey's hands were rubbing Jo's back. Audrey was comforting Jo, just like she did to Ruben. Jo wasn't laughing; she was throwing up!* Brad turned to stare at the red notebook. He ran over and carefully lifted the dollar store pad. Brad sat on the mattress staring at the thing, hardly breathing. *Ruben said read through it,* Brad remembered.

Brad opened to the first page. It said Jo's lists. He smiled and turned the page, to find a list entitled 'Foods I must eat'. The next page was entitled, 'Pills I must take'. Number one on the list was Centrum Prenatal Vitamins. Brad read it eight times.

Jo was frantic. She couldn't find her notebook. She'd looked everywhere. Brad had put it on the counter; she'd made sure he left it. She wondered why she'd even given it to him. Maybe I wanted him to read it, Jo thought, *Stupid. That was stupid. He doesn't want kids. I'm pathetic.* Jo poured herself a big glass of milk and spotted Ruben in the barn. *Maybe Ruben has it? He always has my back.* She smiled remembering how happy Ruben had been with Audrey. Her hands caressed her stomach as she said, "Maybe your grandparents will get married. Wouldn't that be nice?" Jo forgot about the lost notebook and sat down to make a new list of things she needed to accomplish during the day. Only one thing mattered; winning the race that would be their future. Her baby deserved 'a place of its own'.

Brad arrived at the farm around three. He'd gotten an early start and completed his rounds. He waved to Jo, who was having a light training session with Little Girl. He was relieved to see her using the safer training bike during these sessions. He walked directly to Little Girl's stall and mucked it out, then spread a thick layer of clean hay. All the other horses had been left out in the field, so the stalls were now all clean. He strapped on his tool belt and walked out the back door of the barn, pausing to glance at the stall where they had made love. It brought tears to his eyes.

Ruben had been nervous all day, and he didn't like the feeling. He was a man who'd lived on the outskirts of life, more observer than participant. It was less of an obstacle course out there; the groove of repetition was smoother. Now, he was plunk in the middle of real life drama, and he knew it was going to take awhile to get used to the transition. Audrey made it all worthwhile—Audrey and the promise of a grand baby. They both stirred emotions in him that he'd long ago forgotten. He liked what he was feeling, confident he could get used to being involved in life once again.

He'd ridden his horse, Gabriel, up to the farthest pasture to shoot groundhogs. He'd noticed new groundhog holes on his morning ride over to Jo's farm, so he was shooting as many of the rodents as he could find. Ruben had trained his quarter house to sneak up on the animals, then freeze. He'd shot five by the time Brad's truck had pulled down the drive.

Ruben stopped to watch the young man, hoping he was a man of his word. Everything counted on the next moves Brad made. He studied him like a man hunts prey, quietly watching and assessing. When he saw Brad walk toward the meadow, he knew the vet was a man of his word. Ruben kicked Gabriel and headed down the hill.

The weeds had grown wild over the roll of wire. Brad hacked away with his Leatherman knife, and soon the roll was freed. He positioned it next to the rail and rolled out a section. It was blazing hot so he removed his shirt. He squinted as he noticed a rider coming down the hill directly toward him. He watched as Ruben rode up, grateful to see the man.

"Ruben," he said extending his hand, Ruben climbed off his horse and shook his hand. "Congratulate me," Brad said smiling. "I'm going to be a father."

"You have to be here to be a father," Ruben said, looking down to kick some dirt. "You plan on sticking around?"

"I'm gonna be the best damn father I can be, that's for sure. I just can't figure out how to make it all work yet," Brad said leaning against the pole.

"Ya gonna marry Jo?" Ruben asked, looking across the pasture to spot her.

"I'd like nothing more than to marry her," Brad said. "Will you give us your blessing?"

"Ain't mine to give," Ruben said with a smile. "Does she know you know?"

"No, not yet. I have a few things to figure out. I was hoping you'd have time to talk. She'll get suspicious if we just stand here. Will you hold the wire while I nail?"

"Yup," Ruben said, as he threw his weight against the roll.

"How'd that little woman ever get this much fenced in?" Brad asked.

"She flies around this farm like a fart in a whirlwind," Ruben said laughing.

"I've been offered a position on a 2500 acre, thoroughbred farm in Australia," Brad said. "I could take her and the baby with me. Do you think she'd go?"

"Yup," Ruben said. "If you ask her. Even if she had to live on someone else's land in someone else's country."

"I don't know what else to do. I don't have enough to buy the practice," Brad said.

"I heard that," Ruben said, rolling more wire off the roll."

"I know she loves this farm," Brad said. "So do I. I can't imagine taking her off this place. She loves you too," Brad added. "Considers you her pop now and then there's Audrey." Brad added before hammering nails. They worked side-by-side for half an hour, Ruben listening and agreeing while Brad talked and tried out different plans. It took that long for Brad to ask Ruben's opinion. "What would you do?" he asked.

"Well," Ruben said stopping to wipe the sweat off his face. "I learned the hard way that when a man refuses to leave, he finds ways to stay."

Brad found himself mouthing Ruben's words, trying to compute their meaning. "I thought that was what I was doing," he finally announced.

"Nope," Ruben said. "You've been planning how to leave."

Brad whipped the sweat off his face and thought about it. Ruben was right.

"Heard you never even told Doc you want to stay," Ruben added, leaning on the wire.

Brad stared at the man and they locked eyes. "Why didn't I?" Brad asked."

"I keep telling you. You're a fool like me," Ruben said, laughing and clapping Brad on the back.

"I got an idea," Ruben said, "nail this bastard to the post."

"What?" Brad asked as he pounded the nails.

"I'm an old horse trader," Ruben admitted. "I'll make you a deal."

"What?" Brad said, forgetting to hammer the nail.

"Jo's pop let me build my place on five acres. He wanted to deed it to me, but I told him it was too late," Ruben said, nudging Brad to start hammering.

"If I had asked for the land earlier, Audrey and I would have been married over forty years by now," Ruben said taking his hat off and whipping the sweat off his head. "I broke it off 'cause I thought I didn't have anything to offer her." He shrugged. "Turns out all she wanted was me."

Brad shook his head in support.

"I want to buy ten acres of this farm. I don't have much money, but I got enough for a fair price. I raise and breed quarter horses," Ruben said smiling. "I've got a stallion that would give Coco a good time," he added, with a long low chuckle.

"I've been wanting to breed Coco, but Jo said Gabriel's a gelding," Brad explained.

"He is. Couldn't bring a stallion on Hero's turf. Wouldn't be right," Ruben said. "I've got Coco's dream boy back at the farm."

"Sounds perfect. I want to give Jo a horse so we can ride around this farm."

"You have to be here to ride around the farm," Ruben pointed out. He watched Brad's shoulders drop. Ruben reached over and patted his shoulder saying, " I think I have a solution. I want to give you forty thousand dollars. I got more than enough for that."

"Ruben, I don't own this farm," Brad said astounded.

"You will. Jo will go along with this, but I got requirements," Ruben said. "Better hear me out."

"Anything," Brad said. "I'd give you anything, if it meant we could stay here."

"Jo said Audrey and me could be the baby's grandparents. We both want that a whole lot," Ruben admitted.

"I don't have any parents," Brad said with tears in his eyes. "It would be like having you for a father. I haven't had a father since I was six."

"Yeah, I thought about that too. That's what I want," Ruben admitted. "But there's more." Ruben added. "You can't tell Jo anything about you knowing about the baby till after the race. You know that, right?" Ruben asked with a nod. "While we're on that, you better give me the red book. She's been tearing up the house looking for it. I told her I took it 'cause I did," he said, holding up one finger to point out that it was true. "I never lie to nobody."

"Brad reached into his back pocket and transferred the red book back to Ruben.

"Why can't I tell her I know?" Brad asked.

"Right now she's focused on the race. Leave her that way. She needs to do this or she'll never be completely happy," Ruben explained.

"But I don't think it's safe for the baby," Brad said.

"I know, but that's one stubborn woman over there. You'll just cause more problems if you fight it. Right now she thinks the race is the only way to save this farm. She needs to feel that to face her fears. She scared to death of the race," Ruben explained.

"I didn't know," Brad said.

"Audrey met with the doc; he says the baby's the size of a kidney bean right now. It's constantly moving, has little webbed fingers already," Ruben said with a look of enchantment.

"Webbed fingers?" Brad said. "Is that normal?"

"Yup, that's all normal. About this big, I reckon," Ruben said, holding his fingers apart. The two men stared down at Ruben's dirty, rough fingers and they both smiled.

"It's a miracle," Brad said, tears in his eyes.

"Ain't it though," Ruben said whipping his own tears away with the back of his arm.

Twenty

A few days before the race, Jo went to the doctor's office. "Everything looks just fine," he assured her, "How are you feeling?"

"I'm tired. I run out of energy. I have to force myself to make it through the day," Jo admitted.

"That's to be expected. It's the hormonal changes. Right now you're having a dramatic increase in progesterone. Are you experiencing nausea?"

Jo nodded yes.

"Well, vomiting uses up energy. Are you having trouble getting a good night's sleep? Do you have to get up during the night to pee?" he asked.

"Yes," Jo admitted "several times a night, and then I can't get back to sleep."

"I recommend you rest today. No more work. Your race is on Monday, isn't it?" the doctor asked.

"Yes, I don't have time to waste. I leave for the racetrack tomorrow morning. I've got to push through until after the race," Jo insisted, almost panic-stricken.

"Sometimes, our bodies know what's best. You have to learn to listen to yours. If you don't, you might lose more than a race," the doctor said, raising one eyebrow.

Jo's eyes opened and she shuddered. The doctor smiled and suggested, "Let your body build energy for your big day. Maybe your horse could use a day of rest."

Jo looked up and smiled. "I think you're right. We've both been working hard."

"I imagine you're looking forward to the race," the doctor said.

Yes, in some ways, I am," Jo said and suddenly tears rolled down her cheeks. "I'm sorry," she said taking the tissue offered by the doctor.

"Being emotional is normal too. You're growing a baby. It's hard enough work, and I heard the news. It must be upsetting," the doctor said, patting her back.

"What news?" Jo asked, startled.

"Doc sold his vet practice. You'd told me who the father was, remember?" the doctor explained.

"He sold his practice?" Jo asked, suddenly confused. "When?"

"A few days ago," her doctor said. "I thought you knew, or I wouldn't have mentioned it."

"I'm glad you did. I wouldn't want to hear it at the racetrack," Jo said, her tears gone. Her eyes squinted as she tried to understand. Brad had been so happy lately. She'd even heard him singing in the barn while he mucked out stalls. "How did you hear about it?" Jo asked.

"It's the topic of discussion all over town. No one knows who the new vet is. Its got people convinced that it must be someone coming from far away or he'd have met someone. When they ask Doc, all he says is, 'There will be a formal announcement coming soon.' People don't like that," the doctor added. He looked over at Jo and shrugged. "I'm sorry."

"So am I," Jo admitted, "but I wouldn't want to be the last to find out. Thanks for letting me know. I think I'll go home and take a long nap. I've a race to run and I want to be strong."

When she pulled into the driveway, she saw Ruben and Brad laughing together, and she felt physically ill. They both walked over to greet her, and she held up her hand to stop them. "I'm taking the day to rest. Ruben, please take off the tape on Little Girl's legs. Let her roam free in her pasture with Nanny. We're all taking the day off. Brad moved toward Jo, a look of concern on his face. "Don't," she said with a threatening glance.

Rowdy came bounding from around the barn, a flopping, bleeding bullfrog in his mouth. He ran directly over to Jo and plopped it on her feet. Jo gagged. She leaned forward and had her first episode of projectile vomiting. Brad and Ruben stood back, shock on their face. Then Brad ran toward her. She raised her hand and squinted her eyes, wiping her face on the sleeve of her white blouse. "I'm sick. I need to rest in bed. No one, I mean no one, should bother me. Everyone stay away," she demanded as she stared at Brad. Jo stepped out of her vomit-covered flats. Brad watched her walk toward the farmhouse, on tiptoes, like a ballerina dancer.

Jo pulled off her soiled clothes and threw them in the sink. She filled it and let them soak. She stepped into the shower and let the warm water wash away both the vomit and humiliation that had covered her. The water refreshed her, made her feel new again. She rubbed a cake of soap over her body, her hands stopping at her breasts. They were sore and enlarged. She moved her hands down to her stomach; a little pouch had started. She smiled. "We have the whole day, youngster," she said out loud. "Let's make the best of it. Let's sleep and I'll stop dreaming about the race, Brad, and the farm. Let's sleep and plan all the things we'll do together once you're born."

Jo dried off, rinsed the clothes in the sink and hung them over the shower curtain rod. She walked over to the windows, pulling them closed and yanking the shades down. Jo walked to the bed, pulled back the covers and let herself sink into a wonderful, sound sleep.

At seven o'clock, Jo heard a knock on her bedroom door. She sat up and ran toward the bathroom, closing its door to pee. Then she walked over and opened the bedroom door. Brad stood in her living room, a bouquet of flowers in his hands, a big grin on his face.

"I love you very much," he started. Jo squinted and held up her hand, stopping him. She walked over to him, pushing him toward the front door. "I know, Brad. I've heard that before." With strength she hadn't known she possessed, she shoved him out the front door onto the front porch. She stopped at the doorway and screamed, "You love me, no matter how far you may go." Jo slammed the front door in his face.

Brad stood there dumfounded until he heard the door lock click.

The truck was packed by the time Ruben arrived. He stood quietly watching Jo. "Here's a list of things I need Brad to bring over to the fairground. I don't need any of them until tomorrow. If Brad doesn't intend to come, I'll have to ask you to bring them over. Do you mind?" Jo asked, smiling over at Ruben.

"Anything for you," Ruben said.

"I know that, Ruben. Doc sold the practice, probably why Brad's been smiling so much. He's leaving. Hasn't had the decency to tell me about it—doesn't matter. I've got more important things to think about," she said, touching her stomach. She looked up at Ruben saying, "Right Grandpa?"

"Right," Ruben said, grateful that the baby was all right.

"I want to get to the fairgrounds while it's still relatively quiet. I can get Little Girl and Nanny settled, so they feel safe; then they'll enjoy watching the fair come to life," she explained. "Little Girl seems more rested today. It was a good thing to take a day off."

"Yup," Ruben said.

"You promise you'll be there at the race? You and Audrey?" Jo asked.

"Always. We'll always be there for you," Ruben promised.

"Good," Jo said taking in a deep breath. "I love you. I don't tell you that enough."

"No need," Ruben said. "We're family."

"Yes," Jo said, as her hand caressed her stomach again. "You'll need to bring Nanny to the gate during the race."

"Yup," Ruben said. "Audrey's gonna take video. She thinks she's real good at it."

Jo laughed. "I can see her once the baby comes."

"Lots of video from now on," Ruben said, smiling.

They loaded Little Girl into the horse trailer, Nanny following close behind. Ruben waved as she pulled out of the driveway. "Good luck little ones," Ruben whispered.

It had been a smart decision to arrive early. Little Girl and Nanny needed the time to settle into their new quarters. Once they were fed and watered, they settled down and watched the action outside their window. The rides didn't open until after eleven so they were eased into the ensuing chaos. By the time other horses started unloading, they were prepared to see and smell anything.

Nanny was captivated by all the new smells of food. Every hour it seemed a new vendor started cooking something else to tantalize the goat. Occasionally, she bellowed, Ma, Ma, like a little kid asking for a treat.

Jo relaxed in the bag chair she had set up beside the stall door. As the owners and drivers arrived, she rose and enjoyed discussions with her peers. It was a pleasant day until Fred Herman pulled Jo aside, his face showing his anger. "Jo, I just heard some bad news," he said, watching her expression.

"I know. Doc's sold his practice," Jo said putting her hand on her friend's arm.

"No, not that," Fred said. "Sam Randolph isn't going to race against you with one of his own horses. He's going to try to break his own record. He's riding a big stallion out of a farm in Ligonier."

"What?" Jo asked.

"This horse is fast. It's been winning at the fair tracks," Fred warned.

"That's not what we agreed to," Jo demanded. "I said he had to race me fair and square."

"He said you bet you'd beat him on any horse he rode," Fred said, his eyes watching her.

Jo looked away and thought back. "I did say that," Jo admitted. She looked back at Fred and asked. "Can you get the times for the other horse's race and its name. I don't want Sam to see me scurrying around like he's got me unnerved. I'm going to sit here and keep reading my book."

"I have my computer in my truck. I won't tell a soul. I'll copy down all the information I can find," Fred promised. "You remind me of your dad. He and I would always do things like this." He turned and walked away.

Jo settled back into her chair, slowing her breath and calming her nerves. She knew it was only a matter of time before Sam Randolph came her way, no doubt followed by a crowd of onlookers.

Sam Randolph didn't show up all morning. Jo read all the times on his stallion. It was fast and running faster each race, but Sam had never ridden him before. The horse's name was Bruno of Gathers, a huge steed, who liked to race on the rail, first out and staying in front. Fred had found a way to talk to the horse's usual driver, enjoying being Jo's spy. He'd discovered that the driver was miffed that Sam had convinced the owner that he'd have a better chance at breaking the track record since he was the one that held it. As a result, the fired driver had given Fred all the horse's peculiarities, and Jo had developed her own plan for the race.

Brad arrived by noon, sullen and quiet as he approached Jo. He was surprised again as she smiled and pulled him into the stall, pretending to show him something on Little Girl.

"Listen carefully," Jo said her eyes flashing. "Sam's been at it again." She turned and looked out the stall door. "I expect him to come here any minute to announce that he's riding Bruno of Gathers. Here, take these notes! Fred looked up everything on his computer. I think I made a plan to beat that bastard. Here's my plan. Take it away from here and check it over. Then keep it all out of sight." She stopped and looked into his blue eyes. "Thanks for coming, Brad. I love you too—no matter what happens."

She smiled and walked out of the stall, sitting back down on her chair and picking up her book.

Brad took a deep breath, thinking *She still loves me. Thank God.* He shook his head and chuckled. *She is a force to be reckoned with.*

Brad returned with a few suggestions to Jo's plan and a cup of cold milk in a metal coffee cup. He also had lunch in one of

Audrey's plastic containers. They smiled at each other. "Join me at the picnic table?" he suggested.

"Do you feel better?" he asked.

"Much," Jo said. She looked up and warned. "I might throw up again; it's just the flu." Brad smiled and moved down the bench a few inches. They both laughed.

"You've got a good plan," Brad admitted. "I have a suggestion."

"Anything, partner," Jo said biting into a zucchini bread and cream cheese sandwich."

"Bait him. Sam has pinned himself into a corner. If he doesn't win, he'll look the fool," Brad suggested.

"You're right," Jo said, smiling. "I didn't think about that."

"He expects you to ride the rail. He's in for a shock," Brad said, feeling comfortable again.

"Yes, he is," Jo said, taking a drink of milk.

"Bruno of Gathers likes to lead from the front, but Sam might panic and take him out too fast. Then he'll run out of steam," Brad explained. "I studied his times on each quarter. He reaches his top speed at the three-quarter mark. The stallion's times decrease after that, but he's so far out in front it doesn't matter. His jockey told Fred that he has to hold him back during the race to keep some steam in his tank. I saw that on Fred's notes."

"That's right," Jo recalled.

"When Sam comes, look real nonchalant. Listen to whatever he says and then just laugh. Bullies hate to be laughed at. Tell him that it just doesn't matter; Little Girl's times beat his old record."

"Will he fall for it?" Jo said.

"I think she is better," Brad stated. "Really Jo, our horse is going to beat that record."

"From the outside?" Jo asked.

"Because she'll be on the outside." Brad explained.

"I see where you're going," Jo said. "Sam is desperate. He'll push the horse too fast, and then Little Girl will take him from behind."

"You got this one," Brad said. "Sam has no idea what he's in for."

Sam Randolph waited until after six to make his play. All the drivers had arrived; the stables had been buzzing with the gossip. Jo had added to the drama by calming several infuriated drivers down saying, "It doesn't matter; I've got the winner."

Brad was talking with another driver, a few stalls from Jo, as Sam and his entourage walked past. He stepped in with the crowd, eager to see the show.

"I heard you think you still got the winner," Sam Randolph said, forcing Jo to look up from her book.

"I beg your pardon?" Jo asked.

"You heard me. You bragged that you have the winner," Sam shouted.

"Oh that. Yes, Sam. I have the winner," she said and looked down at her book.

The crowd erupted in laughter.

"Did you hear who I'm riding?" Sam asked infuriated.

"Everyone's heard who you're riding. You've spread that news like flies spread crap," Jo said, smiling up at Sam. The crowd moved closer, enjoying every moment of the banter.

"Do you know his times?" Sam spat.

"It doesn't matter," Jo said standing slowly and stretching. "My horse is already running faster than your old record. It's a done deal." Now the crowd was buzzing, not laughing. It sounded like bees gathering in to swarm.

"Let me look at this wonder horse," Sam said, walking over to Little Girl. Nanny bellowed Ma Ma as he approached. The crowd laughed again.

"This isn't the horse you're riding, is it?" Sam said with a sneer.

"Let me introduce you to Little Girl, sired by Hero, the horse who would have the record today if you hadn't crashed into us," Jo announced.

"This thing couldn't beat a donkey. Look, it's got to have a goat. Does the goat run faster than the horse?" Sam sneered.

"No," Jo laughed. "Little Girl will beat any jackass that rides Bruno tomorrow."

"You're a lier. Who's seen this thing run faster than my record?" Sam demanded.

"I have," Brad said, as he walked out of the crowd.

"I don't believe you?" Sam said stepping back. "Prove it."

"I put my money where my mouth is. I saw this horse run and I bought into her. I own half of this winner," Brad said proudly. The crowd buzzed again.

"How'd you pay for it, services rendered?" Sam yelled. "I hear you're penniless—too broke to buy anything." The crowd grew angry and impatient.

"I'm penniless now," Brad said, calming the crowd and reigniting the laughter.

"Watch it, Sam" Jo said, infuriated. "You forgot to pretend you're drunk. You've no excuse for acting like a prick." The crowd roared with laughter and then turned to walk away, leaving Sam alone and unsupported.

"You're both liars," Sam shouted over the crowd. "That thing's too little to beat anything."

"Haven't you heard," Brad said as he put his arm over Jo's shoulder. "The best things come in small packages."

Twenty-One

There were twelve harness races scheduled for the next day, with at least seven horses running in each. That meant over eighty-four horses had owners who were more concerned with their own races than with Sam's threats. While the conversations turned to other subjects, Jo and Brad were careful to keep their distance from each other. They ate separately, never leaving Little Girl and Nanny unprotected. Sam was capable of anything now that he faced defeat. Late in the evening they did sit on separate sides beside the stall, watching and listening to the families strolling the midway or screaming on the roller coaster. Around ten, Little Girl and Nanny grew tired of it all and lay on the hay cuddled together. "I'm jealous of those two," Brad admitted.

Jo looked in the stall and smiled. "You're a born matchmaker."

"I'm jealous of those men with kids, too," Brad admitted. "Look at that man with the little boy. They're having so much fun together," Brad said watching. "Kids are the best,"

Jo admitted, "I'm surprised you're jealous. You're the man who doesn't want kids. You said you wouldn't sleep at night."

"I'd be sure to teach my kids how to keep safe, and you've got me convinced that I'd like a few—maybe four," Brad said, as he smiled at Jo.

"Four would be great. Even numbers, not one or three. Then there's no odd man out," Jo explained, showing she'd thought about it before.

"How many years apart?" Brad asked. "What's optimum?"

"Two," Jo said, smiling, "if everything else makes it possible."

Brad was about to address that very situation when Fred walked quickly up to their stall, reporting, "Great job today, Jo. You too, Brad. Sam's been fuming ever since, walking up and down the other three rows of stalls and talking like a crazy man. He's making a fool of himself."

"Fools can be dangerous; they don't have anything to lose," Brad said looking over at Jo.

"What can he try?" Jo said shrugging. "He's all talk and nobody's buying what he's saying."

"I agree with Brad. Be careful tonight. I see hatred in that man's eyes," Fred warned. "I think he's still vindictive against your father."

"What?" Jo asked sitting up. "Tell me, Fred. Why does he hate me so much?"

"Not you, your father," Fred said quietly. "Not many people know the story. Your dad didn't want to cause any more trouble."

"Tell us," Brad urged.

"Years ago, your dad heard some scuttlebutt about Sam experimenting with drugging a few of his horses. One of the kids that worked on Sam's farm quit because of it and told your dad. He said Sam would run the horse clean, then run the horse the next day with some drug in its system. He was tracking how much they improved and what worked best," Fred said. He paused and looked around, making sure no one was listening. "Your dad loved horses. You know that, Jo," Fred continued. "He hated cheats or liars."

"Like Ruben," Brad said nodding his head.

"Those two were more alike than most brothers," Fred agreed. "Anyhow, Ruben and your dad broke into Sam's barn where he kept all the evidence. Then they copied it and put the originals in a sealed envelope. Gave it to me in case they both got shot or something."

"Fred looked into the wide eyes of the two young people and said, "Yup, it's all true. The two of them confronted Sam. They told him since they grew up together, they wouldn't turn him in, but they'd be watching him. First sign of drugging and they threatened to turn in all the evidence that they'd put in a safety deposit box."

"What happened?" Jo asked. "Did they let him off that easy?"

"Either Ruben or your dad timed every race he ever ran. He knew it too," Fred said. "We never told anyone 'cause they had Sam scared to death."

"Does he know you were in on the truth?" Brad asked.

"No. He doesn't even know that I still have all the evidence," Fred said smiling. "I was gonna turn it in after your accident, but your dad told me not to. Said he'd caused enough trouble for you. I think he knew he was sick," Fred said.

"Did Ruben ever say anything more about it?" Brad asked.

"Not until today. I called him and told him what happened with Sam. He told me to tell everything to the two of you," Fred said. "What you gonna do?"

"Jo and I will have to think about this awhile," Brad said. "Thanks Fred. You've been a good friend to Jo's family."

"Grew up with Ruben and her dad. Played football with them," he said, as he walked away, still lost in memories.

Jo was quiet, until she announced, "I don't want to do anything with this right now. If I do anything before the race, he'll say I just wanted him disqualified. I won't let him off that easy. Besides, too many years have gone by for them to press charges on just that envelope."

"Yup," Brad said.

Jo looked over at him saying, "You've been hanging around Ruben too long." They both laughed.

"I'm going to sleep on a cot in front of this stall, I've slept in worse places," Brad said with a tilt of his head. "You go sleep in the Silverado Inn as planned."

"Thanks; I am tired and we're booked to run in the second race," Jo explained.

"If Sam tries anything during the race, we'll file charges against him—expose everything we've got on him," Brad said with his teeth gritted.

"Good Idea. Do partners kiss when they say goodnight?" Jo asked.

"Not if they're you and me. We can't seem to stop at one kiss. Besides, look how many eyes are watching us," Brad suggested.

Jo stood up and stretched; then she turned and waved to all the other grooms and drivers who were looking their way.

"I'll take you up on that offer after the race," Brad promised.

"You sticking around long enough for that?" Jo asked.

"Yup. Win or lose," Brad said with a wink.

Jo felt her heart flutter, and she smiled saying, "I'd like that."

Three-thirty in the morning, Jo heard Little Girl neighing, kicking and rearing frantically. She opened the truck door and ran toward the stall. The cot was empty; Brad was gone and so was Nanny. Jo moved slowly, raising her voice over her terrified horse's neighs. "It's all right, Little Girl," Jo said firmly. "Nanny just went for something to eat." Little Girl's eyes were wide with fear, her breathing heavy and labored, but she settled down at Jo's touch.

Several owners ran to the stall, talking in the slow cadence horse people knew to use around terrified horses. "What's up?" one asked.

Brad was supposed to be sleeping here on this cot. He's gone and so is Nanny, Little Girl's goat. Something's very wrong," Joe explained keeping her voice even and expressionless.

"I saw Brad pull out about fifteen minutes ago. Heard his phone go off and figured he had an emergency," a woman groom explained. "I got up and went to the bathroom. Came back and heard this going on."

"Call him; maybe he's got the goat," an older man suggested.

Jo called and Brad picked up on the second ring.

"Brad, where are you?" she asked.

"Sorry, there's a barn on fire in New Freedom. There are horses in the barn," Brad explained.

"Wait Brad, I think you've been baited. Someone came and let Nanny out. Little Girl is frantic. Call the number back that called your cell. If I'm right, they won't answer. Then come back here as fast as you can," Jo urged.

The crowd stood motionless, processing all the information. "Spread the word to anyone awake," the old man ordered. "Everyone find that damn goat."

Jo dialed 911 and reported the loss. The police called back a few minutes later. They'd found Nanny, two blocks from the fair. Someone called the police because a drunk was knocking over their garbage and calling out for his ma. They were shocked to find the terrified goat; they were still trying to catch it.

"Give me the address; I'll send our vet," Jo said with a relieved sigh.

Brad returned twenty minutes later, accompanied by two police and Nanny. The goat was prancing like Little Girl, heading quickly to their stall. Little Girl relaxed when she saw her, licking her goat with her long tongue from head to foot. "Fascinating," one groom said. "I've got a horse that needs a goat."

"To hell with the goat, I need a man with a tongue like that," another groom declared. The crowd broke up, laughing as they went.

Brad suggested Jo get back to sleep. She did so after her trip to the facilities. Brad spoke to the police and they promised to question the carneys. "Carneys cause or see everything that goes on in the fair," one explained. Brad asked the police officer to watch the stall for a few minutes.

He walked around to Sam's camper, knocking on the door. Sam staggered to the door, looking sleepy. Brad pushed his face within inches of Sam's and he growled, "If you were dumb enough to use your own cell phone to call me, you're in big trouble." He turned and stomped away, his fists balled up.

The benefit from the night's activity was that it took the focus off the race. Jo was mad, but no longer nervous. She was more determined now than ever to beat Sam Randolph. Little Girl was so happy to have Nanny back that nothing seemed to throw her.

Ruben, Audrey and Nanny walked behind Jo and the racing bike as Little Girl headed onto the track. They stayed beside the gate where Little Girl could see Nanny each time she ran past. Jo was the first driver to pull out onto the track. She wanted Little Girl to get a few laps in because of her two days without exercise. Little Girl was excited and relieved to be able to run. She seemed to hold her head higher, lift her feet quicker. Jo had trouble holding her back to slow her down. Sam was the driver of the second horse to enter the racetrack. He smacked Bruno with the reins urging him to run full speed to catch up with Jo.

"Stupid idiot," Jo thought with a knowing smile. As Sam passed she could hear his fake laugh, but she also noticed how big the stallion was. "He looks like Hero," Jo said, and she grew furious.

The first warm-up lap around the track, Nanny called out to Little Girl and the horse increased her speed. Jo pulled back keeping Little Girl in a trot. Sam had lost all horse sense. He was whipping Bruno so that he would lap Jo.

"Good," Jo thought. "Wear your horse out."

All seven horses had entered the track; all had been warmed up, so the announcer gave the signal and all the drivers slowly turned their horses the racing way. The car with the starting gate pulled in front of the uneven line of horses. They moved behind it, the horses allowed to find their own paces for the introductory lap. Sam brought his reins down on Bruno's back insuring that the stallion would be the first introduced. "What an ass," Jo thought. "She listened as they introduced Little Girl, driven by Jo Martin, owned by Jo Martin and Brad Kirby of Hobby Hill Farm." She would never forget that moment.

As the truck and starting gate pulled around to the back straightaway, all the drivers lined up in a row, their horses' hooves pacing quickly to keep up with the now speeding truck. At the starting line, the gates swung closed and the truck sped away from the line of racing horses. Jo heard Sam screaming, "Get," as he whipped the reins against the stallion's sweating body. No other driver had yet to bring their whip on their own horse.

"Sam's a mad man," Jo realized. The field of horses watched as Sam and his stallion sped ahead of the other horses. They all ignored him, keeping to their individual plans for the race. The first time around Sam's horse was running far ahead, full speed, sweating and breathing heavily. The crowd was not impressed, more aghast. Sam never sensed their disapproval.

As Jo and Little Girl ran the last turn in the first lap, Nanny bellowed Maa, Maa, and this time Jo let Little Girl speed up. The horse raced past the stands with her feet flying and the crowd stood in excitement. As she passed the turn where Sam had crippled Hero, Jo shouted, "Go Little Girl" and touched her on the left flank, urging her to the outside. Little Girl responded, wild-eyed and irritated with the horse in front. Jo touched her back lightly with the whip and kicked the racing bike, their signal to let it all go. Little Girl took off, lifting the crowd to their feet again as the small horse took on the giant stallion.

As they ran on the back straightaway, Little Girl heard Nanny bellowing, Maa, Maa. The horse's eyes grew wider and her feet went into a pace that even Jo had never expected. Little Girl passed Sam and his exhausted horse. She was in the lead as she passed Nanny, Ruben and Audrey. The determined horse charged past the stands crossing the finish line as the winner of the race.

Five horses finished before Sam, leaving him to finish with an exhausted, defeated horse. Jo turned Little Girl and began her lap towards the winner's circle. She passed Sam, who lifted his whip to force his horse into Jo's line. The horse ignored him, dropping his head and heaving for breath.

Jo breathed a sigh or relief and headed toward the viewing stands, the crowd still on its feet screaming. She pulled up Little Girl as Brad, Audrey, Ruben and Nanny came running onto the track. They all hugged, delirious with pride. Nanny and Little Girl were nuzzling noses. The crowd watched, fascinated.

The announcer remained quiet, checking something with the statistician. Finally he called for order, saying, "We have a new track record. The winner, Little Girl, her driver Jo Martin and owners Jo Martin and Brad Kirby of Hobby Hill Farms have just broken the track record with a time of 1 3/4 minutes.

The crowd reacted with applause and cheers. I have a few more announcements the speaker informed them. The films will be reviewed for possible charges against Sam Randolph, driver of Bruno of Gathers. Someone handed the announcer another piece of paper, and he read it and smiled. "I've been asked to announce that Brad Kirby, part owner of Little Girl, will be the new veterinarian and owner of Doc's practice.

While the other riders and owners in the stand went wild, Ruben and Brad looked at each other and nodded. The photographers' flashes continued for ten minutes. The pictures would stand on their mantels for generations to come. Ruben and Brad were down on one knee, each holding little blue ring boxes opened for inspection by the two gaping women above them. Behind them, a goat and horse were licking each other.

The End

Read on for an overview of the
Living Passionately Series

I hope you have enjoyed reading Racing Desire as much as I did writing it. It is the perfect book to start my new **Living Passionately Series**.

Each book in the **Living Passionately Series** will be a story about a woman who is enthralled with the vocation she has chosen for her life's work. The women will be very different but share certain attributes. They will each be imperfect and vulnerable. They will enjoy living in the flow, embracing all life's experiences without hesitation. When love enters their lives, they will run toward it, enthusiastic partners in the exploration of all its mysteries. These women know that only through connections are we truly alive.

The Shepherd's Hook

The second book in the Living Passionately Series is entitled, *The Shepherds Hook.* Join Bess and her five-year-old daughter, Sadie, as they settle into their new life in Pennsylvania after the death of Bess's husband. Bess is enjoying her job as an instructor at The Mannings, which supplies everything a knitter, weaver, or spinner could require. When Bess and Sadie meet the shepherd who provides the fleece Bess spins, they are all sent whirling into an adventure that will take your breath away.

The Shepherds Hook is due to be released in February 2014. Until then—Live Passionately!!!

Pamela H. Bender

About the Author

Pamela H. Bender's life has had many twists and turns, not unlike her novels. She says her life has unfolded like chapters in a book, each one teaching her a great deal about people living different human experiences. Always a writer, she has noted the details of their various lives and in the case of Racing Desire, the animals they live with. Racing Desire was written over twenty-eight years ago. She put it on a shelf but never forgot it. Once her first three books were published—Until There Was Us, Rising Up, and Worlds Apart–she was ready to re-evaluate the old manuscript. The former heroine was weak and easily manipulated. Bender reports that it was cathartic to rewrite the book with a strong, independent heroine who is not afraid to take on the world. "We all evolve and hopefully improve with age," Pam said. "It's the various chapters in our lives that make us who we are." Committed to delivering only strong, interesting heroines, her new series is called Living Passionately. Her next book, The Shepherd's Hook, will be released by Spring 2014.

25182101R10129

Made in the USA
Charleston, SC
18 December 2013